BREATHLESS 6

Drive Me Wilde

by Shani Greene-Dowdell

This is a work of fiction. Names, characters, places, and incidents either are the product of the author's imagination or are used fictitiously, and any resemblance to actual persons, living or dead, business establishments, events, or locales is entirely coincidental.

Chapter One

Tasha

Fired Up

My heart rate sped up. Blood raged through my veins at an astounding rate and pressure that made every part of me feel alert. I saw red. My temples pulsated. This could not be happening.

"Fired? You're firing *me*?" I asked in a low, unbelieving tone that didn't match the explosive volcano of emotions erupting inside of me.

Melinda Lory had the nerve to look at me as if she felt terrible for firing her best writer.

"I'm sorry, Tasha. We gave the head writer position to Nina after she submitted that raving *Hollywood Jailbreaks and Heartbreaks* piece last week. She was supposed to be temporary, but she has solidified her place here, and we just don't need you right now."

More pressure built inside of me, this time slamming into my gut and causing physical pain. I tried to mask the sorrowful look I knew was piercing from the depths of my deep-set brown eyes.

"Oh, you mean to tell me that she's being promoted after she stole my story from me?" I asked.

"Ha! You've got to be kidding me, Tasha. What are you suggesting? Are you accusing Nina of stealing?" Melinda's

3

round red cheeks flew up into a smirk, and she had the nerve to look indignant. She knew very well what I was saying.

"Mel, we both know she doesn't write the type of content that was in that article, and the fact that she's sleeping with Richard is the only reason she can do what she does and get away with it. She's the reason I wrote the story about sexual misconduct in Hollywood, and she's getting promoted to head writer while I'm losing my job. There's nothing right about this," I said in disbelief.

After building my own popular blog, I landed a position writing for this celebrity column for two full years, the longest I'd ever been at one particular nine to five job in my adult life. Before coming to *Colorful Times,* I'd put in my time generating clicks on my blog and growing my following. Lately, I was losing grip on what I created, all because of Nina's sticky fingers.

"Again, I'm sorry, Tasha. Your column just isn't doing good, and numbers are all that matter to the bigwigs. I hate to say this, but maybe you should consider another profession," Melinda said slowly, or at least the words hit me slow…and hard. My eyes nearly popped out of their sockets as the tension from our conversation bubbled over to a climax.

"You have some nerve, Melinda! I'm a damn good writer, and you know it! The only reason my column isn't doing well as it should is that Nina keeps hijacking my stories," I said through a clenched jaw.

"As far as that's concerned, it's your word against hers, Tasha."

"This is so unfair. You know I'm not lying because you know my writing style. Hell, you might as well give her the password to my computer, because Nina is getting my stories to print faster than I can press 'the end' and submit them," I spewed then a wave of paranoia set in, and I started to believe Melinda was in on it.

I'd put the same argument before Melinda when Nina stole her first story from me. That one was a puff piece about Jay-Z and Beyoncé's daughter's stylist, where I showed the stylist's new hair products some love. Nina got her hands on it somehow, and her name ended up on the byline.

This is highway robbery.

"The higher-ups are not falling for your argument about plagiarism," Melinda informed me. "They're not concerned about your bickering either. They only care about what's making money, and right now, you're not it. Listen, I'm just following orders." Melinda looked away from me before returning her dead hazel eyes to mine to say her final devastating words. "Clean out your desk and be out by lunchtime. Your last paycheck will be in the mail."

"This is fucked up," I said as I stood up and stormed out of Melinda's office.

Melinda had to know what Nina was doing. She'd read my stories for two years. She, of all people, should be able to pick my writing style out of a lineup. Still, she let me take the fall instead of Nina, the slimy, opportunistic office pass-around, and I felt hoodwinked. *Good people always get the shaft.*

Without being able to prove Nina hijacked my stories, I had no choice but to pack my things and leave the *Colorful Times* office building, hoping karma would bite all of them in their asses.

I marched across the parking lot to my car, holding the small box with my belongings in my hand. I managed to crank my few years old Chevy Malibu and drive home crying until I couldn't shed another tear. My dream was to become an editor for a high-profile blog or magazine one day, and that hope was dashed by two self-centered, conniving women who were too lazy to squeeze an ounce of creativity out of their brains.

I kept asking God why this was happening to me when I treated other people better than this. By the time I arrived home, I was devastated but had come to terms with no longer being employed. Melinda dealt me a low blow, and I would somehow recover and find a way to stay afloat.

***

Two weeks later, I was done licking my wounds. However, the thought of ever writing another word drained the life out of me. I lost the thirst for storytelling, research, and the chase of the next celebrity mishap.

Instead, I found myself doing what I never thought I'd do—take Melinda's advice to work in another field. It seemed Melinda and Nina's underhanded mistreatment also set another precedent in my life; I became all too familiar with being fired.

I got hired at a local photography studio. Since I liked to snap unique images with my phone camera, I figured I'd do well taking pictures. But it didn't work out that way. Within a week, I was let go.

"Fired?" was the question I had for the overbearing manager when she strolled into the session I was shooting and asked me to come to her office. "Why are you firing me?" I continued.

"You can't tell parents that you need a wide-angle lens because their kid has a big head, Tasha," she reprimanded me while giving me the side-eye.

"Well, he did have a big head. I was only trying to get the whole thing on the picture. It wouldn't look right if I took the picture with half of his head on there, would it?" I argued my point to no avail.

The manager didn't see things my way. She could have spent a little time showing me how to adjust the lens to take a good picture of this kid somehow, but, instead, she sent me back through the doors she'd invited me into, permanently.

Next, there was the independent coffee house, Nayberry Cafe. I didn't believe it would be that hard to make coffee. After all, it was coffee…not gourmet dishes. However, staring at the contraption with buttons, nozzles, and steam maker attempting to make a mocha something, I felt helpless. I yelped when I dropped yet another cup of the hot liquid on the floor.

"Holy cow, Tasha. This just isn't working out," the frustrated owner was livid, though I could tell he struggled to talk to me in the calmest voice he could muster. "The cup is too hot for you to hold because clear plastic cups are for cold drinks," he said.

"My bad. I think this cup was in the wrong spot," I said.

"Look, we've given away too many complimentary beverages because of your mistakes. You're fired," he said quickly, before stripping me of my apron and telling me not to come back.

By the fourth firing, I was harshly reminded that answering one's cell phone instead of ringing up groceries was unacceptable. "I know, I'm fired," I told the manager before he could say it. Yeah, I knew the drill by then. I was fired from the grocery store that day, but not before I had been so lucky as to ring up the mega-bitch, Melinda's, groceries.

"Tasha, is that you?" she'd asked with so much shock and awe in her voice as our eyes met. I thought she would orgasm right in the middle of the grocery store from seeing me ring up groceries; the sight appeared to cause joy to resonate from her soul.

I didn't respond. I scanned her goat cheese, salad mix, and alkaline waters as quickly as I could so that I could get her out of my space.

"Well, I'm happy that you found work," she said as she slid her card to pay for her groceries.

A sigh was my only response. Melinda sounded sympathetic, but I knew she was gloating. Part of me wanted to reach across the counter and knock the smirk out of her.

"Thank you, ma'am. Have a great day," I gave her the greeting I gave all of my customers and moved on to the next person in line. A few minutes later, my line slowed down. I sneaked my phone out of my pocket and called my best friend, Dana. "Girl, I'm about to lose it. I may need bail money if I see this bitch again," I spat out when she answered.

"Wait, what happened?"

"Melinda just came through my line throwing shade at me and, ouuuh, it took everything, including the blood of Jesus, to keep me from scratching her face."

"Melinda came in there?" Dana asked, sounding as shocked as I was.

I could feel my temples pulsing. "Yeah, she just left."

"That shady weasel! Someone had to tell her you were working there. It's too much of a coincidence for her to show up at that store and go through your line. She lives all the way in Broward County," Dana informed me; her usual soothing tone sounding suspicious.

"You know what? I don't even care. I'm done with all of this. I feel like walking out right now." I was already selling myself short by taking the job as a cashier instead of working to revive my writing career. However, I just couldn't see myself writing again, not a single word, if it was that easy for my hard work to be stolen and my credibility erased as Nina had done.

Dana broke into my thoughts, which were quickly heading in a downward spiral. "I may have something better for you, anyway. Meet me at our spot at seven tonight, so we can have drinks and talk about it."

"Okay, see you then, Dan—a." I was about to hang up when my boss walked up behind me.

"What's going on here, Tasha?"

Startled by the sound of his voice, my eyes focused on the line of customers that was so long that it was starting to go down one of the food aisles. An elderly gentleman stood in front of me with shaky hands, barely hanging onto his walker, waiting for me to check him out. I slid the phone into my pocket and opened my mouth to speak.

"I know, I'm fired."

"No, just clock out and take the rest of the day off," my boss said firmly.

"I can ring them up," I offered.

"No, go ahead and finish your call, and I'll take over your register." The manager held one hand out as if asking me to move from the spot in front of the register.

I clocked out and left the store holding my head high, knowing this was the end of job number four. My phone rang on the ride home, and my boss officially relieved me of my duties after taking ten minutes to think about it. He let me know I should not return the next day and when to expect my last check. *Four jobs in two months. You go, Tasha!*

I went home that evening and just thought about giving up. Maybe I'd become a ward of the state and live off government assistance. Hell, there was no use in working. I was only going to get used or fired.

Maybe I was the problem. Maybe I had done something so vile and disgusting it was just time for karma to rain down on me and make me atone for my past sins, whatever they were. I thought I treated everyone pretty decent, but perhaps there was a bad omen hanging over my head.

I knew that was BS, though. Nina and Melinda were just threatened by me working in that office. They knew if I were ever to get the writing credits I deserved, I'd run that place, and they'd be the ones out of a job. They were probably laughing their asses off, knowing I was out of the industry and bouncing around from job to job.

I showered and changed out of my khaki pants and grocery store tee-shirt into a comfortable romper and slide-ins before going to meet Dana at our favorite Cuban restaurant. She was inside, waiting for me when I arrived. She was seated close to the back but still in view of the doorway.

"Hey, Dana," I greeted when I reached our table.

"Hey, Tasha, how are you, love?"

"Girl, the most I can say is I need drinks. Lots of them."

She laughed as she slid a mojito in front of me. "I already ordered for you because I knew you would want one."

We sipped our drinks, and I made humor out of the past few months of my life. "So, here I am. I've gone from potential lead writer of a world-famous blog to being unworthy of ringing up groceries. Oh, how the mighty fall. Cheers!" I tilted my glass toward Dana and took another drink.

"Girl, I'm still seething about Mel and Nina. Those are some sneaky bitches. They make me want to suit and boot up and go up in there and kick their asses. That, or sneak them; I know where they live, and I have black masks and gloves. We could roll on them at any time."

I laughed and waved her off. "Nah, I'm not trying to let them take me down any further, but if we run into each other again, I can't tell you what I might do. Ski masks, though?" I laughed again. "You're crazy, and that's why I love you."

"Damn right, I'm crazy when it comes to my family and friends. But, neither of us would look good in orange jumpers, so we'll just have to settle with knowing Mel and Nina are going to get what's coming to them one day, and I just hope we'll get front row seats when someone sues their asses for plagiarism." She smirked and added, "I wish you would sue."

"All I want right now is to be able to make a paycheck. I can't worry about a lawsuit that may or may not pan out."

"Well, I can tell you now, the reason you're not making it in these jobs is that you're not supposed to be doing them. You're a writer, and I hate they made you feel less than that."

"That waxes poetic in my mind and all, but unless I start my own freelance business, I'm pretty sure Melinda has blackballed me with every credible employer in the industry. She gets a kick out of rubbing elbows with other editors and gossiping about whatever's hot that week. Plus, I'm pretty damn sure I can't use her as a reference. That's just my reality right now," I said.

"What about the success you had with your blog before you went to *Colorful Times*?" Dana asked.

"It's all rolled together at this point. I just don't see myself writing again, Dana."

"Well," Dana spoke thoughtfully. "I have an opportunity that could hold you over financially until you can find your way back into the writing field. A new celebrity lawyer client of mine needs a part-time sitter asap, and the pay is very good at two grand a month for mainly afternoons and some evenings, with a bonus for weekends when he's out of town on business."

"That money does sound good, but a sitter? What, for his dog?" I cringed. "You know I don't like animals like that. I wouldn't make it a day."

Dana snorted. "No, it's nothing like that. He has custody of his nephew, and he's looking for someone to be there when he's working or away on business." Dana let that marinate, gauging my response to the business card she handed me.

I wrinkled my nose at the card. "Sitter? I don't have any children, and I don't know a thing about babysitting. I've spent time with my little cousins, but I've never actually kept them by myself for any long period of time."

"You didn't know anything about photography, coffee, or groceries either, yet you earned a few dollars doing it," she pointed out.

"Well, we see how well that turned out." I laughed.

"You're right, but Matt is a good person. He'll be patient and work with you. He's just looking for someone he can trust. I trust you with my life, so I know I can refer you and feel good about it." She looked at me with genuine eyes. My beautiful friend with long flowing black hair, perfect little nose, cheekbones that celebrities pay for, and smooth brown skin resembled a glowing angel as she smiled at me. A smile that was code for 'I'd better not mess this up.'

"Thank you, Dana. I know you love me, but—"

She put her hand up to halt me from continuing. "Just don't fuck it up, okay?"

"That's what I worry about with any job right now. I'm starting to feel like I can't do anything right." *Take pictures, make coffee, ring groceries—and I definitely can't protect my copyrights.*

"Well, if there's one thing about you, Tasha, it's that you have a good heart. That's the main thing that is needed in caring for a child. You'll figure out the rest once you get there. I mean, how hard can sitting with a ten-year-old be? All you have to do is be nice, let him do what he wants, as long as he's not doing anything harmful, of course. You can handle this with no problem, Tasha. I know you can," my friend hyped me up, and I was starting to believe I could, indeed, be responsible for another human for hours at a time.

"Oh, ye of much faith," I purposefully misquoted because Dana believed in me so much. Tilting my glass to take another sip, I thought long and hard about her offer. She was asking me to do something I'd never imagined doing—be responsible for someone else's kid.

"I have faith in you, my friend. You have had some bad experiences lately, but I want to give you a chance to get things back on track in your life. This is some excellent money, and you'll be around a celebrity lawyer and may even get the inside scoop on some things to pique your writing interest back up. But listen, you know I aim to impress my clients with the utmost professionalism, so I know you won't do anything to get fired or to tarnish my reputation of recommending the best of the best people." Her response was a mixture of a question and a statement.

"Are you seriously depending on me not getting fired, after losing my last, I don't know, say ten or eleven jobs? I think the jury is back in. Me and people don't play well together."

"Tasha, just make it work. For you and me, please..."

"Alright, Dana, for you, I'll try. It's not like I don't need the money," I admitted and emptied my glass while staring at the card.

In the pit of my stomach, I felt this job would end in a hat tilt just like the others had. Then, I would go live in the endless black hole of failure that had become my life. This time, I would not only have let myself down. I would also be letting Dana down.

Have a little faith, Tasha. A tiny voice pushed through the growing cynicism rooting in my spirit. I was going to try for Dana...and for my landlord's sake.

"Be there tomorrow, and don't be late," she told me.

14

"I'll be there, just tell me what time."

No one in my circle of family and friends, other than my best friend, Dana, knew I had been job-hopping since being let go by the lucrative celebrity blog I helped build. I didn't tell my Aunt Clara or Cousin Destiny that my column got hijacked and stopped generating money, because of the influx of content thieves and new blog columns similar to mine. I had been thrust back into the workforce and trying to find a spot that fit me. So far, nothing I'd done with my creative writing degree had worked out for the long term, and I was at my wit's end.

When I came out of my thoughts, I noticed Dana scrolling through her phone.

"What are you doing?" I asked.

"I'm trying to get Matthew's schedule organized. His name is Matthew Wilde, by the way. He has several out of town meetings coming up, so he will need you to be with his nephew quite a bit over the next month. That's if you guys hit it off at the interview tomorrow. I'm looking at his schedule so that I can schedule you a time for the interview." Dana was a personal assistant to people with pockets deep enough to pay her for tasks that would seem effortless to most people, like keeping one's schedule in order, making sure their meetings start on time, and setting reminders for important events. Her motto was, 'your time is your money, so leave the petty tasks to me.'

"This job requires an interview?" I was getting nervous again. "No, Dana, I don't want to mess this up for you."

"Every job requires an interview, silly. And, stop thinking about messing up. You messed up on your other jobs because you didn't have your best friend's reputation on the line," she said, and her well-sculpted, pecan colored face went deadpan. "So, this is different. More is at stake."

"I know."

"So, be there at eleven tomorrow with a resume, and make that money, girl."

"I've got you, Dana." I hoped I was right as I gulped down yet another drink.

I wanted nothing more than to live up to my word and not make a mess of working for Dana's client, Matthew Wilde. I desperately needed to make enough money to cover my monthly bills. The more I thought about it, the more I figured sitting with one of Dana's client's snotty nose nephews couldn't be *that* bad.

Chapter Two

Matt

Boys Night Out

The noisy diner echoed the sounds of the customers as I glanced at my nephew, Cody, and watched him take a bite of his French fry. I was reminded every time I looked at him of how much he looked like my sister, Marisa. Sure, he had some features of his father, Tony, but mostly it was Marisa I saw when I stared at him. I remembered the day I got the call that his mother had been killed in a car accident. When I arrived at the hospital, the devastation continued. His father also didn't survive the wreckage. Along with the heart-wringing hurt of losing my only sibling, the enormous responsibility of raising her son landed in my lap like a huge boulder. A duty I never shirked and took on with love and compassion from day one.

Cody looked up at me, and his face held a smirk.

"What Uncle Matt?" he asked, casting a shady grin that I'd come to recognize.

I shrugged. "Can't an uncle look at his favorite nephew?" I grabbed a fry from Cody's basket, popping it into my mouth.

Cody rolled his eyes. "Of course, since I'm your only nephew." His sarcasm rang loud and true. "Just looked like you had a faraway look in your eyes. That's all." He casually took a bite of his sandwich and glanced in my direction.

At ten years old, he was *far* too smart for his own good. Of course, it helped that he had to grow up fast...too fast for my liking. I didn't want to tell him I was thinking of his mom. It had been two years since the car accident, and not a day went by when I didn't think of her. Cody seemed to be the stronger of the two of us, and I hated putting that pressure on him.

"Eat up, so we don't miss kickoff," I said, chuckling as I politely changed the subject. He didn't seem to notice the switch up as we finished our meals quietly. When done, I threw some money down on the table, and we got up to leave.

As Cody's sole guardian, I made a point to make time to hang out and bond with him. Unfortunately, those times were few and far between. As a celebrity lawyer, I was forced to go where I was needed, and that left me with very little time for ball games and fun trips. Business tended to take the forefront of my life, and personal obligations seemed to fall by the wayside. I was in dire need to feed my social life, so I looked forward to the times I could get away from the daily grind. One day soon, I planned to take Cody to Colorado to ski as I promised him we'd do this holiday season. With his good grades and even better behavior at school, the little man deserved some time on the slopes and lots of time playing in the snow. If I were truthful with myself, I'd admit I needed a real vacation that wasn't work-related, as well.

Cody and I made our way to the door. I opened it. He stepped outside. I spotted a gorgeous woman heading in. She looked at me and smiled. I nodded my head in greeting. Her big brown eyes glanced over me, and I noticed her caramel-toned face warm up to an even brighter smile. She moved past me. I casually glanced towards her, mentally making a note of her plump ass as it swayed towards the counter. I chuckled and shook my head, then walked outside. When I looked at Cody, his eyes were searing a hole in me, and he held that smirk again.

"What?" I asked him.

"She's mighty fine, don't you think?" He winked at me, and my jaw dropped.

"Mighty fine? Boy, where do you pick up on these things?" I wrapped my arms around him, and he laughed as we went off to my car.

"I'm not a kid, Uncle Matt. Believe me...I know all about women looking good. You need a woman like that in your life."

He nodded meaningfully for emphasis. It was my turn to roll my eyes and laugh as I got into the driver's side of the car. Cody slid into his side.

"First of all, my man," I started. "I need no such thing." I glanced at him before starting the car. "Something you'll learn soon enough is that women are only trouble."

Cody raised an eyebrow. "Well, that's not what all the older guys at school say. They say that a man and woman need to get together so they can have babies."

I chuckled then glanced at my impressionable nephew. The last thing I wanted was for him to be carrying the weight of needing to procreate on his tiny shoulders.

"Men and women don't *need* to get together to have babies until they're at least forty or fifty, so you have plenty of time to think about that, buddy."

Cody leaned back in his seat and shook his head.

"Whatever you say, Uncle Matt." The sly smirk on his face was proof he was far advanced beyond his years. It was only a matter of time before I'd need to have *'the talk'* with him, and maybe sooner than I thought. I turned around and started the car, thinking about what Cody said.

I wanted to believe, ever since he started living with me full-time, I'd been the role model Marisa and Tony hoped I'd be. I was careful not to bring women home, though most of Miami perceived me as a ladies' man. Since Cody moved in, I had only had sex with three women. To me, that was saying something. It had been two years, and men had needs, but I didn't want Cody to think sleeping with different women was okay. I also wanted to build a bond with him. I didn't want him to feel he wasn't good enough for me, or that I had to crowd our space with a harem of women. Little did I know, he thought it was a necessity to have a woman in my life.

We drove the rest of the way to the stadium. The jam-packed parking lot was full of football fanatics ready to take in the high school football game. It was the Bulldogs vs. Ravens, and we had our money on the Ravens. Okay, so we weren't betting men, but we were rooting for them. It was my alma mater, after all, and where Cody would one day attend high school.

We got out of the car, and Cody immediately started asking questions. "You went here, right?"

"That is correct, my man," I responded proudly. "For four years, I was a dedicated Raven. I was on this very football field many Friday nights."

"Whoa..." Cody murmured with gleaming excitement in his voice. "Were you the quarterback?"

I chuckled. "I hate to disappoint you but no...not exactly. I was a wide receiver."

There was a long pause while I waited for his response. He shrugged. "Oh...well...that's an important position, too."

I nearly laughed at the way his disappointment rebounded through his compliment. "Come on, my man." I patted his shoulder as we entered the gate, paying for two tickets then walking toward the bleachers. "Want something to eat?" I pointed to the brightly-lit concession stand. "There's a small line now, but if we hop in, we can avoid the rush that's going to come later. Do you want popcorn...cotton candy?"

Cody held his stomach, amusing the hell out of me. "Way too early to discuss food, Uncle Matt. Maybe later."

We went to the home side to find seats. This kid kept me either smiling or laughing at something he said or the funny expressions he made when he talked. As I looked around to find us a good seat, Cody pointed in the general vicinity of two empty ones. I followed him to wherever he was pointing, and we went up the bleachers to take a seat next to two women. The moment I sat down, I could smell the strong fragrance of the perfume on the lady next to me. She smiled, quirking her pink painted lips upwards. I politely smiled back then glanced at Cody. He was giggling with his hand covering his mouth, which only meant one thing. He'd conveniently picked these seats to place us next to the women.

I sat back to enjoy the game. Kickoff happened right on time. I watched Cody and smiled as my mini-me couch-quarterbacked beside me, calling plays and jumping up and down with excitement when our team made a good play. I wasn't doing poorly when it came to raising him, but the last two years had been a struggle for me, a self-proclaimed forever bachelor. I never saw myself as a family man before I adopted Cody, but he made me see myself in ways I couldn't have imagined.

We cheered for the home team with yells and claps, our enthusiasm matching the Ravens as the wide receiver intercepted the ball and ran it all the way back for a touchdown. At half-time, we were up by fourteen. I turned to Cody and asked, "Do you want something to eat now?"

"I want some nachos, but we'll lose our seats if we get up, so I can stay here and keep our seats?" he put to me as more of a question.

My little man. This was another moment that made me proud to be his uncle. He was growing up fast and becoming such a responsible young man. I still couldn't get over the fact that he was in double digits. I didn't recognize any faces in the packed stadium, but I wanted Cody to know I trusted him to take care of himself for a short time while I grabbed our food. I nervously looked around at the crowd, then slowly turned back to him.

"He'll be fine. I'll look out for him," the lady with the pink lipstick offered, batting her lashes.

"Thank you, ma'am." I felt a little more at ease. "You can stay here, Cody, but do not move from this spot," I warned him.

Cody smiled while nodding. "I won't move an inch. I promise, Uncle Matt."

I hurriedly made my way through the thick crowd to the concession stand. Once I worked my way to the front of the line, the worker asked, "What can I get you, Hon?"

She was twirling her finger in her hair as she ogled me with a hint of desperation in her ocean blue eyes. It made me uncomfortable, so I focused my attention on the menu hanging overhead.

"Give me two nachos and a medium Coke," I answered while flashing her a warm, platonic smile that screamed 'see you at church Sunday' and not 'I want to see you naked.'

"That'll be ten fifty." She held her hand out for the money.

I dug my wallet from my pocket, handing her the money. My phone buzzed with the sound of a calendar update notification as the lady's fingers lingered in mine. I pulled my hand back, fetching my phone out of my pocket and opened it. The announcement had come from Dana letting me know of a nanny interview the following morning. She also placed a message on the meeting notes that the candidate was a good friend of hers who was highly recommended. Given Dana was highly respected and had also come with excellent recommendations, I trusted her word. Still, I needed to talk to this person to make sure we'd be a fit.

Maybe this one will be the one. I heaved a sigh. With my workload getting heavier and engagements stacking on top of each other, I was running out of time to find someone.

Smiling, I thanked the woman behind the counter who was holding out the nachos and drink to me. Then, I headed back to Cody, sighing in relief when I spotted him sitting where I left him. Giving Cody his nachos, we watched the rest of the game, which the Ravens pulled off with a thirty-two to twenty-one win.

As we were leaving the stadium, I observed my little man. He was a good kid. I just needed a little bit of help with taking care of him. I had to do right by him, so hopefully, I would soon find the right person to provide the loving care he deserved whenever I wasn't available.

Chapter Three

Tasha

First Impressions

I pulled into the long, winding driveway at the address Dana gave me. Getting out of my car, I looked up at the modern-style brick home that was huge enough to be a mansion but small enough to fit into the neighborhood of upper-scale homes. I walked past a silver-toned street model Harley parked in the middle of the walkway and smiled. I always wanted to know what it felt like to ride a motorcycle like this but never had the chance, and more importantly, the nerve. At least, I'd get the opportunity to watch my new boss ride away on it, well, if I could get past this interview and get hired.

Sighing, I knocked on the door. A tall, brown-haired man opened it, and wow, he was good looking. It should be against the law for any human to be that handsome. *Stay professional.* Crossing the line would be effortless; he was a better-looking version of Clark Kent, and damn him for making me feel warm and fuzzy inside. His eyes were deep brown and masculine, yet friendly. There was a slight stubble on his chin, creating a gorgeous five o'clock shadow. My mind immediately imagined kissing him and feeling that stubble against my softer face. He also had a dimple in his right cheek as he grinned, and it made me go a bit weak in the knees. The

25

aura of the man standing in front of me gave me mental retribution for all the months of writing from sunup until sundown while neglecting my personal need for romance. Matthew Wilde was romance in human form.

But I wasn't there for romance, and definitely, this visit wasn't personal. I swallowed the lump in my throat to speak instead of standing there looking lost...and probably like a complete lunatic.

"Hi, I'm the Tasha, I mean the sitter. No, what I meant to say is that I'm here to interview for the babysitting job." I took short breaths in an attempt to calm my nerves after a collage of words seemed to rush out clumsily.

He cleared his throat and stepped back so I could enter into his home. "Glad you made it on time. That's a plus since I have to leave in about an hour. You can come with me." He turned around. My eyes landed on his backside, and I inwardly groaned. *He has a nice ass!*

Tasha control yourself. You're here for a job, not to check out asses, I chastised silently. But I was a goner. I officially had a reason to lose job number five in record time, probably day one—sleeping with the boss. I internally slapped myself to knock sense into my unemployed mind and body. I had bills to pay, couldn't afford to fall for Matt. Lord, why am I calling him Matt in my thoughts? I meant, Mr. Wilde.

I followed him into his study, panting on the inside to calm my nerves. He motioned for me to take a seat in the chair across from him. I did so, all the while thinking I needed to get it together. My emotions were all over the place, mainly lustful and impulsive ones.

"Do you have a resume for me?" he inquired, quirking up an eyebrow.

"Of course," I choked out and focused on answering the interview questions. A slow breath released as I handed over the resume once clutched inside my hand.

Mr. Wilde nodded as he took it from me. He scanned over the resume, giving me time to glance around the study. It was a huge, nicely decorated room that appeared bigger than my studio apartment. Actually, the hallway we walked down to get to this study was probably bigger than my apartment. I smiled, then Mr. Wilde cleared his throat. I quickly snapped my attention back to him. His eyes bore a hole through me; my resume was lying flat on his desk. Oddly, I felt awkward and comfortable at the same time. *How long had I been admiring his beautiful décor?*

I crossed my legs, which caused my skirt to inch up a little more on my thigh. Mr. Wilde's eyes gravitated to them and widened. My smile grew wider; I had his attention now. *But you don't want his attention. You want his job.* I had to keep reminding myself of the reasons I was there—Dana, a job, and my landlord.

Mr. Wilde cleared his throat again and started looking over the resume once again. Barely glancing at the first page, he asked, "Tell me, Tasha, what qualifies you for this job?"

I didn't plan for such a serious question right out the gate. My mind went blank. The only thing I could do was speak from the heart. If he didn't like what I had to say, then he wouldn't like me. *Don't blow it, Tasha...*

"I have a lot of passion and heart," I began.

The oversized brown leather chair creaked as he crossed his legs and leaned back in it. His intense gaze pierced holes through my eyes as he looked into them, waiting to hear more.

Every person looking for a job has passion and heart, I scolded myself. I had to come up with a better reply.

"What I mean is when I want something, I go for it, and I put everything I have into it. It's the same thing I will do if I have the opportunity to work with your son," I said sincerely.

"Nephew," he interrupted me.

My face turned a thousand shades of brown. "Oh yeah… I'm sorry, nephew; I knew that," I mumbled.

"No need to be sorry. It's a common mistake. Go on," he invited.

"Mr. Wilde, I will treat your nephew as if he were my own. That you can be certain of." I hoped that didn't sound cliché. "I would never want to let you down."

His eyes widened.

"I mean, I wouldn't want to let anyone down and especially not a child entrusted in my care."

He smiled and let out a small chuckle.

"Do you have any experience?" he asked.

"I have experience working," I said and giggled slightly. *Dang. Stop laughing.*

Mr. Wilde's smile held up, but he didn't laugh with me.

"With children?" he iterated.

"I don't have any experience working with children, but I love children, and I'm confident I can handle the job. I would love the opportunity."

His eyes scrutinized each word, causing me to twitch in my seat. *Do I really love children?* I wondered as the warmth from his glare spread through my inner core. With the way I reacted to Mr. Wilde, I could love his nephew as much as he wanted me to love him. Honestly, I would do anything to be in his bed right now, but that would so defeat the purpose of the reason I was there, needing a job.

Mr. Wilde's orbs captured my soul, and his look alone was enough to make beads of sweat appear on my skin. Each glance from his hooded eyes caused me to tremble with a need I didn't know was there. Biting my lower lip, I denied words from escaping that I shouldn't be uttering.

"It's like this," he started, shifting slightly in his chair.

I waited patiently to hear his rejection. Instead, he looked me over, stopping at my thighs with a lasting and longing gaze.

"Please don't take this the wrong way, Tasha, but you don't look like a babysitter," he concluded. "What interests you about this job?"

My cheeks puffed into a blush. I took what he said as a compliment, and it was showing on my face. But should I have taken it that way? I mean, how does a babysitter look? Not looking like a babysitter could be the nail in my bill paying coffin. I needed Mr. Wilde to feel confident I could do this job.

"Mr. Wilde, with all due respect, I don't think you'll find someone that will work harder than me, regardless of what a babysitter should *look* like." I paused because the next words out of my mouth might be more honest than he could handle. "The thing that interests me the most about the job is what motivates most people—being able to pay my bills."

Ha! My past managers would say otherwise. I shook my head slightly, trying to remove the annoying voices from my mind that reminded me of my recent firings.

"I won't let you down if you give me the chance to show and prove it," I added confidently.

"I will give you a chance," he said, nodding. "But not because of your past work history alone. I will give you a chance because I trust Dana's recommendations. Plus, your background check came back fine."

"Background check?"

"Yes, I had Dana send me more information on you so I could at least do a criminal background check before you got here. I pulled a few strings and got the information I needed this morning. Your record is clean, and your past employers gave you good recommendations in the area that matters to me most—your character," Mr. Wilde admitted.

"I don't have a record, and though it didn't work out with me being a writer, photographer, barista, or cashier in the past, I will take good care of Cody. I'm good with grammar and writing, so I could help him in those areas," I asserted.

"Let's try it out for a couple of weeks. The past nannies have come from an agency, but your background is clean, and I know Dana wouldn't give her word unless she trusted you. She says you are a good friend to her, and a friend of hers is a friend of mine." He stood up from his chair. "So, what I'm going to do is start you out on a two-week trial period, and we'll see how it goes. Once I'm sure Cody is comfortable with you, I'll offer you the permanent position with benefits and everything."

Oh, my gosh! I got the job! I'm going to be able to pay my bills this month. I internally gushed.

"So, let me show you the house," Mr. Wilde said before giving me a quick tour of his house and introducing me to a bubbly, young Cody.

"Your home is beautiful," I commented as we walked toward the front door. "Goodbye, Mr. Wilde."

He stopped in his tracks, chuckling. "Where are you going? You have to babysit." He extended a card to me with his cell phone number circled.

"You want me to get started now? As in today?" Not expecting that, I was slow to take the card or close my mouth, which was gaped wide enough to catch flies.

"Yes, I have a few meetings to attend. I was going to let Cody tag along, but how about you guys hang out for a few hours and get to know each other?" he suggested.

"O—kay." Stammering, I looked back at Cody, who was just as surprised as I was.

Before leaving his ten-year-old nephew in my care, Mr. Wilde gave me the rundown on his petty cash, what Cody could and couldn't watch on TV, and that he needed to go clean his room asap. I honestly couldn't believe it happened that fast.

For the first fifteen minutes after Mr. Wilde left, I stood in his foyer, trying to get a grip of this surreal moment. I was officially a babysitter. What a difference a day makes, eh?

I quickly texted Dana to tell her the news. Then, I had work to do. After quickly Googling fun babysitter games, I chose the safest and most fun one. When Cody came downstairs from cleaning his room, I proposed, "Hey, let's have a pillow fight."

Cody's eyes lit up with surprise, and he smiled brightly before running into a downstairs bedroom. He came back out with a handful of pillows, which after thirty minutes of abuse, became undone, spilling their guts around the living room. We had tons of fun, and everything went well for the rest of the day, except for a few 'minor' hiccups.

When Mr. Wilde called to check on Cody, he told me he would be out longer than expected. He spoke with Cody, who assured him he was safe and enjoying our time together.

I found more fun activities for us to do, just like the pillow fight. I ordered a pizza with the cash Mr. Wilde left for us, and Cody and I were sprawled out on the floor coloring in books when a deep, angry voice startled the two of us.

"What the hell happened in here?" Mr. Wilde growled. A wild look of utter confusion covered his handsome features with doom. On his call, he said he'd be home at six, but it was only four p.m.

Gosh! I had intended to clean the mess up before he got there. Cody was even going to help me out. It was going to be the final project of the day. I jumped up from the floor and opened my mouth to explain, but Cody beat me to it.

"Uncle Matt, we had so much fun! We played with the pillows, and they exploded, and Tasha burned the waffles, and the fire trucks came when she made a big fire outside, and there was smoke, then she pushed the grill in the pool and then—"

I didn't exactly expect Cody to tell him *everything* that happened in one breath, but it was the truth. I only ordered pizza after my pan of waffles exploded on the gas grill. I had dreamed up the bright idea to cook waffles outside while Cody played solo football, tossing the ball in the air and catching it.

"Cody, why don't you go brush your teeth while I talk with Tasha." The look on Mr. Wilde's face made me nervous. I was sure I'd blown this for not only myself but for Dana. It was bound to be my fastest firing yet. "The fire department?" he asked.

"Ah, well, yeah...I didn't need them to come. Cody called them. I guess I used too much lighter fluid on the grill."

"Lighter fluid? It's a gas grill, Tasha."

"I figured that out after the fire department came."

The slight wrinkling of his forehead turned into a harsh frown, and I felt like I was a kid who was about to get yelled at by her parents. I anxiously looked around at the mess, and a sick feeling overcame me. The den area looked like a wrecking ball hit it. When he looked at me, there was so much disappointment in his eyes, and I knew then that wrecking ball was me.

"I don't think this is going to work out," he finally said.

My mouth hung open. "So, I'm fired?" Again.

It was clear that was happening, but I hated to think I was already out of a job I had barely started. *Was today even a workday? Damn, I don't want to have to look for another job.* Nothing seemed to be going my way lately.

"I'm not saying that you are fired, but I do need time to think about everything that happened here today. I'll call you tomorrow morning to discuss it." Swiping a hand over his mouth, Mr. Wilde couldn't even look at me. His aggravated voice was anything but soothing to my ears.

"Would you like me to clean up? It was the last thing that I had planned to do today, and it's the least I could do."

"No, thank you. You've done enough here."

"You're right." I walked out of his home with my tail tucked between my legs.

Spending the day with Cody gave me so much life. He made me feel young and vibrant again. His company took my attention from my past failures and hard knocks in life and just allowed me to be carefree Tasha. We enjoyed ourselves to the fullest without any constraints or responsibilities. If nothing else, I met myself again as I interacted with an innocent ten-year-old who unknowingly gave me hope. I'd planned to get up the pillow contents and straighten the house before Mr. Wilde returned home, but time got away from me. Oh, well. Now that the fantasy of being the sitter for a well-known celebrity lawyer had gone up in smoke, I had to figure out a way to call Dana and let her know screw up number five was officially a done deal for the both of us.

Chapter Four

Matt

A Convincing Plea

Watching her pull out of the driveway, my heart sank. I had to admit it wasn't easy seeing her stand in my face looking devastated as Cody told me everything that happened while I was away. I didn't want to see her go either. The minute she walked into the house for the interview, energy waves flowed from her, making every part of me tingle. My cock twitching in my pants was the result of her beautiful, sensuous body that willed me to respond. She had medium brown skin with long, curly hair that cascaded over her shoulders. When she smiled, her whole face lit up. When she smiled, my entire face lit up. She had just that beautiful of a smile. I warned myself she was there to work and not for my pleasure. I stayed on task for the interview and went with my gut to hire her on the spot.

I walked back into the living room, and my stomach tightened. I had a huge mess to clean up, but I didn't want to work on that just yet.

I remembered looking at her resume. On paper, she wasn't qualified to be a nanny. Her passion and honesty drew me to her. She was feisty, and I liked that in my women. I reminded myself during the interview that I wasn't interviewing a girlfriend; I was interviewing a babysitter. When her skirt hiked up her silky brown thighs, I couldn't get her legs out of my mind. So maybe what I thought was my gut was lust, since everything else pointed to her not being the right person to care for Cody.

I shook my head and looked at the mess once more. I should have let her clean up before she took off. She was right about it being the least she could do. I groaned, then walked up the stairs to Cody's room and saw his door was open. I peeked my head in; he was lying across the bed coloring.

I knocked softly on his door. "May I come in, buddy?"

"Sure, Uncle Matt." Cody sat up on his bed and showed me the picture he was coloring. "Do you like my picture?" I never saw him that excited about coloring before.

"Yeah, I like it a lot. You did a good job on it." I joined him on the bed. "Listen, I wanna talk to you for a minute. It's about Tasha."

"Isn't she awesome?" he asked.

It felt like the wind deflated from my chest. He wasn't going to take the news of her not sitting with him any longer well. I could tell he wasn't going to go for me firing Tasha, but I had to break it to him.

"Yeah, bud, she's awesome." A flash of her sweet smile during the interview clouded my mind. "But you see, the thing is…she's not going to be coming back. I'm going to have to find you another sitter." *One that won't burn the place down, and set me on fire, as well,* I thought.

Cody leaped from the bed.

"What? What do you mean she's not coming back?" His eyes were wide, and he looked angry enough to bite my head off.

"It just didn't work out," I stated, having put my physical attraction to Tasha aside to come to the most logical conclusion.

"What do you mean it didn't work out?" His fists went to his waist, and he glared at me. "She was the best, Uncle Matt. You can't do this to me," he argued. "This was the best day of my life! I want her to be my nanny. I haven't had anyone like her around me since mom passed away."

Hearing him speak of his mother in that way hit me where it hurt…my heart. I lifted my eyes to his, and he had tears in the corners of his eyes. Tasha's lively energy had affected us both in the short time we knew her, and it would be great if she could stay. I had warmed up to the thought of having her around, and if Cody took to her so well, then it was a tough call. I couldn't imagine leaving her with Cody again. If something tragic happened while he was in her care, I wouldn't be able to live with myself. Seeing how she left the house, it's plain to see she wasn't in control while I was away.

"You saw how messy the house was," I started laying out my argument. "Your other sitters may have had things we didn't like about them, but they all kept the house neat and didn't set anything on fire."

Cody nodded. "Yeah, but the house is messy because we were having fun. The others only cleaned up and made sure everything looked good for you. They didn't care about my favorite colors or talk to me about my favorite superhero like Tasha. None of them talked to me and asked about my feelings like Tasha." Cody paused for a second, visibly calming down. "Uncle Matt, what if I clean up the house? Can she stay?"

I chuckled. In the two years I had custody of Cody, he never once offered to clean the house.

"It's not only the mess; she nearly burned the house down, buddy. You had to call the fire department. Who knows what would happen next?"

"She had already put the fire out. I just got scared and called them," he confessed. "She didn't tell me to."

"I don't know, Cody. It's still a bit much that happened on her first day. Imagine her second and third days with you. Things could get wild." I imagined the things Tasha could set ablaze if she stayed longer—namely me.

"I'm sure she's learned from her mistakes," he reasoned. "She understands me, Uncle Matt. I say I don't like Brussel sprouts, and she's not going to push it on me."

I snickered. "So, in other words, she won't make you eat healthily?"

Cody shrugged. "She understands that I'm still a kid. Surely, you can get that. I just met her, and I don't want to lose her. Please don't fire her. None of these other babysitters will treat me nice like her. I just know it."

He was fighting hard for me to agree with him, and what was even worse was I was starting to. There was just one problem. I told Tasha I would think about it, but I was sure she figured I was going to fire her. I wasn't sure I wanted to change that position.

"Please," Cody pleaded again, shining his puppy dog eyes towards me, causing me to groan loudly.

"Argh! Fine, Cody, but if she ultimately burns down the house, I'll say I told you so," I griped.

Cody nodded. "Deal."

"And, she will still be on two-week probation. If anything else I don't like comes up, we'll have to find somebody else," I advised him.

"Okay, Uncle Matt." He started towards the door.

"Where are you going?"

"I have a mess to clean up, don't I?"

I rolled my eyes. "Get back here and color another picture like the one you just finished, and I'll clean up the mess."

Cody was excited to get back into his bed to color. I left his room, knowing I had a call to make. It wasn't going to be too easy, but I had to do it. The sooner, the better.

Chapter Five

Tasha

Bullies Beware

I had just gotten up the nerve to call Dana and tell her I blew her good-standing relationship with Mr. Wilde when my phone rang. I looked at the caller ID and didn't recognize the number, so I cautiously answered it.

"Hello?"

"Tasha, this is Matt. I know it's late, but I need your help." The sound of his voice sent shivers down my spine and caused my stomach muscles to clench.

"Mr. Wilde, how may I help you?"

"No, please call me Matt."

"Okay, Matt, what can I do to help you?"

"You can accept a second chance to work for me. I do need a sitter that can step right into the job, but Cody loves you. He hasn't accepted anyone the way he has you. You're all he has talked about since you left."

I wasn't fired…yet. It took quite a few breaths to control my enthusiasm building. I was excited for two reasons; I didn't have to disappoint Dana, and part of me wanted to see Mr. Wilde again—I mean, part of me wanted to see Cody again.

"I would love to come back and hang with my little bud. And, I appreciate the opportunity to show you I'm much

40

better than what happened today. It was my first day as a babysitter, and I got carried away with the fun activities and didn't spend as much time on the responsible tasks. I understand that now and will change that completely."

"Great. I'm glad to hear that, and I'll have someone over to prepare meals for you guys, so you don't have to cook. You should have no reason to touch the outside grill, okay?"

"Yes, sir. I won't let you down," I assured him. He was giving me this second chance, and that was more than any other boss had given me.

"Okay. See you on Monday?"

"Yes, and thank you for this opportunity to come back and work for you," I said sincerely.

"Just please...don't make me regret it," he verbalized with a stiff voice.

"I...I won't," I stammered, understanding his ambivalence. After all, I started a fire at his home while having the life of someone so precious to him in my hands.

"Alright. Have a good night, Tasha. I'll see you Monday. Please pick Cody up from school at 3:15. I will text you the details." Before I could respond, he hung up.

I sat back and let out a deep sigh.

About thirty seconds later, the text with Cody's school address came through. I glanced at it and pushed the phone off to the other side of the bed. It was true that I had a great time with Cody, and I didn't want that to end, but I needed to be more careful, and I would.

***

Monday, I pulled in front of Manchester Prep Academy at 3:15 sharp. I followed the line of cars picking up their kids and scoured the yard to see if I could find Cody. When I spotted him, it wasn't a sight I ever wanted to see. He was talking to some boy when the boy put his hands up to Cody's chest and shoved him so hard that he had to catch his balance.

My jaw dropped as I watched the fiasco unfold in front of me. Cody just stood there and took it, like he had no other choice. That was when the boy pushed him harder. Cody fell to the ground. I looked around. No one was even attempting to help Cody out. This didn't sit well with me. The boy laughed and walked away, while Cody was in a heap on the ground.

"I don't think so, little man," I mumbled, swerving out of the spot I was in. I grabbed a parking spot in the front and jumped out of the car, only grabbing my car keys to lock the car. Dodging the vehicles coming through the line, I reached Cody.

"Cody?" I called in a low tone, attempting not to bring more attention to him. "Are you okay?"

He looked up at me, his face red and tears in his eyes.

"Hey," he sadly replied.

Cody stood up and moved away from me, but I grabbed his hand and forced him to look at me.

"What's going on?" I questioned softly. My goal was to get to the bottom of it and kick some ass, if necessary.

"I just wanna go home," he whined.

"Does that boy always bully you?"

His face masked over with bravery, but I could see the fear under the surface. "It's really alright, Miss Tasha.

Sometimes, he wants me to bring him money for lunch, and if I forget, like today, he'll try to remind me never to forget."

I knelt in front of Cody. "Little buddy...that is *never* alright. Do you understand?"

Cody nodded, and then I heard laughter from someone standing to my right. I turned to find the bully, along with three other little mobsters, laughing their asses off.

"Wait right here," I murmured to Cody.

"Tasha, no!" he pleaded.

"Trust me! All will be well." I put my hand on Cody's shoulder and squeezed softly, assuring him. Then, I walked off to where the boys were standing.

They saw me coming, and all but one started to disperse, but I was able to stop them with my voice.

"Hey!" I shouted.

Two of the boys stopped and turned to face me. The one that was picking on Cody stood there unbothered like a little gangster. "What you want, lady?"

"What's your name?"

"Bobby Brown, but I'm the new, New Edition," he joked, and his little posse giggled. "What's yours?"

I couldn't believe the balls on this little kid. "Do you think it's alright to pick on others that are smaller than you?"

He didn't respond.

"So, like, for example...if I was to do this..." I put my hand to his shoulder and knocked him back. It was a slight movement that wouldn't have knocked anyone to the ground, but he fell backward.

"I'm telling you did that!" he complained loudly.

I rolled my eyes and knelt so that I was eye level when I spoke to him. "If I ever hear of you bullying my friend Cody again, you are gonna wish you were a roach getting sprayed by Raid instead of me stepping on you," I warned low, speaking for his ears only then cracked my knuckles as I stood back up straight.

The kid with him asked, "Hey, what did you say to him, ma'am? Did she threaten you, Bobby? We can tell the teacher."

I glared at that child, and he cowered away from me. I looked at Bobby again. "No threats, just promises. You don't pick on people, and you don't have to see Miss Tasha again. One day, you're going to remember this little encounter, and you're going to know that I taught you a valuable lesson. No one likes a bully. The bigger the bully, the bigger the fall," I forewarned in an ominous tone. "Come on, buddy. Let's get you home." Turning on my heels, I grabbed Cody's hand, and we walked to the car.

"That was awesome. The way you talked to them, Tasha, I know they're not going to say anything to me again. They keep picking on me because I'm smaller than them, but I don't think they will anymore. Thank you!"

I smiled. "It's what friends do."

The corners of his lips lifted into a smile. "Are you really my friend? We just met."

I shrugged. "I knew right away you, and I would be the best of friends."

He reached out and touched my hand. "It's what my mom would've done. I would love to have a mom like you."

My eyes watered, and I felt like tears would spring from them at any moment as I smiled down at him. "Thanks, little man. I would be honored to have a son like you."

I squeezed his hand then turned to back out of the parking spot. I was emotional from hearing his words, and I meant every one of mine. If I were lucky enough to have children, I'd want them to be just like Cody. He was a sweet child with a warm soul. As long as he was in my care, I would do anything to protect him. Handling a bully was only the beginning.

Chapter Six

Matt

Hot Seat

The phones were ringing off the hook. My assistant, Mary, was running around like a chicken with her head cut off. This was the reason I hired Dana to be my second personal assistant. She wasn't as hands-on as Mary, but whatever Mary couldn't handle, she passed along to Dana, along with Dana planning my hectic daily schedule. It was a very busy Monday, and I barely had a moment to breathe all day long. When my phone started ringing, I started to send the call to voicemail, but it was Mary's number on the caller ID, so I answered.

"Hey, what's up?" I solicited while quickly typing up an email.

"Sorry to bother you, Matt, but there's a Dean Westcott on line one. She said she's from Manchester Prep Academy. It sounds important."

I glanced at the clock on the wall. It was just after five. Tasha was supposed to pick up Cody from school, so I didn't know why they would call me two hours after closing. *God, I hope she didn't forget him.*

"I'll grab it, Mary, thanks." I clicked the line over and anxiously said, "This is Matt Wilde."

"Hello, Mr. Wilde." Dean Westcott's stern tone of voice caused me to stop typing to listen to her without distraction. "Sorry to bother you this Monday afternoon, but we need to talk. Can you come to my office immediately?"

I frowned. "May I ask what this is about?"

"We would prefer to discuss it when you get here."

I heaved a sigh while looking at the stack of work on my desk. I could continue to work well into the evening hours, as busy as I was, but this sounded important.

"I can be there in half an hour," I conceded.

"Alright! We'll see you then."

We hung up, and I finished typing up the email, sent it, and logged out of my computer. Grabbing my cell phone, I hurried out of the office.

"Mary, I have to leave. I'll see you tomorrow," I said as I stormed past her desk.

"Is everything alright?" she yelled after me.

I paused at the door and shrugged.

"I don't know. That was the school calling, and they didn't want to talk over the phone, but I'm sure everything will be alright. Pack up and leave, because it's not fair for you to be stuck behind."

By the time I got to my car, I had dialed up Tasha's number. She answered almost immediately.

"Hello?"

"Hey, Tasha…it's Matt." I started up my car and backed out, fumbling with the phone and putting on my seatbelt. "Just got a call from Cody's school. They asked me to come in and speak with them. Any ideas why?"

There was a long silence on the other end of the line. I waited impatiently as she stalled.

47

"Well, there was an altercation at the school when I picked up Cody."

"Altercation? What kind of altercation?"

"Some kid was bullying him."

That was all I needed to hear to go from zero to ninety-nine. As a skinny kid growing up, I was bullied. It wasn't fun; I despised being the one who always got picked on.

"A bully, huh?" I mentioned as a knot formed in the pit of my stomach.

"Yes, and I witnessed it after school."

"Tell me what happened."

She explained how she stood up for Cody, and I listened intently and reflected on the information. I appreciated her caring enough to have Cody's back.

"Cody and I talked, and he said it's been going on the entire school year. What bothered me the most was, with all of the students and teachers out on the school grounds, no one noticed this kid, Bobby, pushing him around."

"I will take that up with the dean, but Cody should have said something to me about this a long time ago," I grumbled, knowing I never said anything when I was bullied as a child. At the time, I felt it would only make it worse. I didn't have anyone like Tasha to stand up for me. "Alright. I'm here at the school about to go in, but Tasha, thanks for being there for Cody. I appreciate it," I told her when pulling into the parking lot.

"Anytime, Matt...sorry, I meant to call you Mr. Wilde," she stuttered as she spoke.

"No, it's fine. I told you to call me Matt, remember?"

"Okay. I'm sorry you had to leave work to go up there."

"You don't have to keep apologizing, Tasha. I'll be home when I'm done here, and we can talk about it then, okay?"

"Alright," she replied softly.

Hanging up, I got out of my car and slipped my phone into my pocket, prepared to find out what I was battling.

***

Dean Westcott peeked out of the office and motioned for me to come inside. With the way she watched me as I walked past her, I felt like I was walking into the lion's den. Her staff hadn't kept a close eye on the car riders, so this wasn't Tasha's fault. I sat down, prepared to tell her exactly that when she introduced the man seated next to the principal. "This is Henry Jackson. He's the head of the school board."

I nodded and shook his outstretched hand. Then, my attention went back to Dean Westcott.

"It's been brought to my attention that there was an incident on the lawn after school today during pickup. Bobby Gentry's mother and father called me, saying they don't appreciate their son being bullied by one of the adults."

"Hmmm..." I sighed, hoping to keep a cool head. As a lawyer, staying calm in stressful situations was my trademark, but when it came to Cody, I had a weakness. "So, you think Bobby was being bullied? Well, that's quite interesting, considering that no one at this school knows who the real bullies are."

Dean Westcott looked astonished by my statement. "What exactly are you saying, Mr. Wilde?"

"My nanny pulled up this afternoon to find my nephew being slung to the ground by older and bigger children. All she did was point out to Bobby that bullies won't be tolerated…and that bully is Bobby Gentry, who has been extorting money from my nephew for God knows how long. I commend my nanny for addressing a situation that has been happening right underneath your noses, and none of you even noticed." I glared back and forth between the principal, board member, and the dean. "What I would like to hear is an apology for the accusatory tone you have taken with me," I demanded of Dean Westcott.

They gave me a look of disapproval, and I could tell that they didn't believe a word I was saying.

"Why would *I* apologize? We don't tolerate adults bullying kids, and you should mention this to your nanny before she's no longer allowed on the school's property," Dean Westcott rebutted, ignoring everything I just told her.

Her raised voice didn't sit well with me.

"So, you don't tolerate adults sticking up for children, but you tolerate other kids bullying and weaseling lunch money out of an unsuspecting gentle-hearted kid?"

Dean Westcott shrugged. "We aren't sure what happened between Bobby and Cody."

"It seems like you're not sure of anything that's going on here. That's why I just explained to you that my nephew is being bullied!"

"We have to look out for all of our children, and adult's harassing other people's children is simply not allowed," the head of the school board spoke up.

"I thought you said you weren't sure what happened."

"Sir—" Dean Wescott began, but I cut her off by holding up my hand.

"Well, it's like this...it seems to me that you all are more concerned about my nanny's actions than the fact that she was protecting my nephew. That's ridiculous, and for that reason, I will pull Cody out of this school without batting an eye," I fumed. "Plus, I have no problem removing all my financial backing to this school, and you know that there's a lot."

"You don't need to do that. We're just saying that maybe you should tell your babysitter to back off," the principal chimed.

I leaned back in my chair, prepared to fire shots at them all. "I think that instead of that, you need to implement plans to reduce the bullying after school. I'm sure Cody isn't the only one. Until then, I'm done here." I stood up from my chair and glanced down at Dean Westcott for a few more seconds. "Stopping bullying is your challenge. Get rid of the bullying, and this school will be better. I doubt my friends with kids enrolled here would appreciate knowing this is going on. And I have no issues with telling them. Maybe they will want to pull their children and funding, as well. Yeah, and telling other parents is just the lightweight part of what I can do. We don't want to talk about lawsuits, racial discrimination against my nanny, or anything of that nature because that part will close the doors to this prestigious school. I would hate to see you go down for taking the word of the parents of a bully over mine, just because my nanny is black. Do you see how I can word this on paper?" I posed.

51

"You don't need to be hasty," the head of the board huffed.

I laughed indignantly. "You haven't seen anything yet. I promise you my words aren't empty." When I reached the door, I looked back at them. "For the record...I stand by Tasha, and she nor I will apologize for her actions. She did nothing wrong." I left the office, leaving the attendees of the meeting dumbfounded.

I hopped inside my car and backed out of the parking lot, ready to get home to Cody and make Tasha aware that I wasn't taking their side. When I entered the house, I found them in the kitchen. Cody was eating the dinner the cook prepared for him while Tasha looked at me with a worried expression.

"How'd it go?" she probed me nervously.

"You won't have any more problems out of anyone at that school. I don't stand for bullies, and I told them they should have the same beliefs. If they don't see things my way, and fast, they will have a problem on their hands, and it's going to be a big problem. No one is going to bully Cody around and be protected by the school officials."

She nodded. "I was so upset when I saw it. I just had to do something."

Her distressed brown eyes made me want to touch her hair, rub the stray strands into place, and run the pad of my thumb across her pouting lips. I refrained from my desire to console her in the way I wanted to.

"I'm glad you were there for him," I said, knowing I'd made the right decision giving her a second chance.

"The cook lady made beef and noodles, my favorite," Cody interrupted.

"Sounds delicious, my man," I said.

Tasha broke me from the moment of admiring her standing beside Cody and me by announcing, "I'm about to head home so you guys can enjoy your dinner."

"Why don't you stay and eat with us? After all, I think we have more than enough food, and it would be my way of thanking you for today." I glanced around the kitchen, and everything was still intact. "Besides, you didn't try to burn my house down today, so that's always a plus."

I laughed so she would sense that I was teasing her.

"Ha, not funny!" she disputed and giggled with me.

"Please, Tasha...stay!" Cody begged. It warmed my heart that he had already grown so attached to Tasha.

She nodded. "I would love to stay and have dinner with you."

"Good!" I went over to the counter to grab two more plates, then turned around and saw Tasha and Cody were deep in conversation. Recognizing she was someone we could both get attached to made me want to take a chance on her and be cautious at the same time.

Chapter Seven

Tasha

Just Can't Handle It

After we got past the fact that I unwittingly got Mr. Wilde sent to the principal's office, things settled into a regular routine of me picking Cody up from school, giggling and talking for a while, getting his homework done and dinner warmed up. I never expected to have a job as a nanny, but Cody was a wonderful kid, and his uncle wasn't so bad either. I could get used to the job, especially working for the hottest bachelor in town. Of course, I didn't speak those thoughts out loud. I stayed on my best behavior, and I didn't do anything to provoke Mr. Wilde into thinking he couldn't trust me. I was a pretty darn good babysitter, despite initially not having any experience.

So, when Cody came to me and told me he wanted to have some guys over after school, I didn't think much of it. After all, I was glad to see him becoming sociable with some of the other kids from school, especially after the incident with Bobby, the bully.

"Sure thing, Cody," was my reply. I was going to be the cool babysitter if it killed me; I didn't know then that it very well almost would.

When I was leaving their house, Matt walked me to the door. "What's this I hear about some of the guys coming over tomorrow?" he quizzed me with a little smirk on his lips, which I found sexy and endearing.

I smiled and shrugged. "Oh, Cody told you already? I was planning to talk to you about it before I left, but it's no biggie. Just thought it'd be a way for Cody to make more friends."

He nodded slowly.

"Ever hang out with three or four ten-year-olds?" he inquired, and the way he was looking at me made me think he had a secret he was enjoying keeping from me.

"Well, no, but how hard could it be? I can take them to get some ice cream, watch them play a game of football, put on a movie. It'll be a piece of cake."

He arched an eyebrow, laughing and shaking his head. "You have no idea what you're getting yourself into, do you?" He snickered, and it was cute to see him laughing at me. "I would pay money to be a fly on the wall."

I frowned. "They're ten-year-olds, not toddlers."

Matt grinned as if I had no clue what I was saying.

I had to prove I could handle a few ten-year-olds. "I've got this, Mr. Wilde."

"Hey, what did I tell you about that?"

"Matt," I backpedaled and playfully patted his shoulder.

A smoldering heat zinged through me as I touched him, causing me to pull my hand away slowly. I hadn't felt that type of energy from a man, and certainly never had a man gaze at me with that kind of hunger in his eyes. I was taken aback by the moment. Slowly backing up, I nearly fell out of the doorway. Matt laughed, making me feel as if my stumbling alone proved I couldn't handle that many boys.

"You don't think I can handle it, is that it?" I asked, my tone low and maybe a little hurtful that he had no faith in me.

He shrugged. "Guess it's not so much that I don't think you can handle it; it's just that I'm reminded of how things went on the first day you were here, and that was with one kid."

I crossed my arms in front of me and gawked at him. "Not fair to bring up the past, Matt. You know I've come a long way since then. I've been here a month, and have I given you a reason to doubt me since the first day?"

He tilted his head, his eyes sparkling with a mischievous grin. He slowly shook his head. "Ummm. Give me a minute to think about that." He paused to think it over.

"Matt!"

"No…you have not given me any reason to doubt you, Tasha. I'm sure tomorrow will be an amazing day," he said sincerely.

"Even if you're being condescending, I will prove you wrong," I vowed. "It *will* be amazing, and it's a shame you won't be here to hang out with us." I smirked before turning to leave. "Have a good evening, Matt."

I honestly didn't think it would be that big of a deal having Cody's friends over, but the next day, I was thirty minutes into the boys' get together and thinking a different story. Four boys, including Cody, loaded up in the back of my vehicle and headed to get ice cream on our first stop. After each got their ice cream cone and took a seat in the booth, things quickly turned chaotic.

"I should have got chocolate," Bryce said.

Jason taunted Bryce because Jason got chocolate ice cream, and that irritated Bryce, though he chose vanilla. Bryce flipped his hand up, catching Jason's cone and knocking it from Jason's hand and onto the floor.

Jason shot up out of his seat and screamed, "Are you kidding me? That was a jerk move."

Bryce stood up to defend his actions. "You shouldn't have been rubbing it in my face."

Cody and the other boy, Max, were eating their ice cream and watching as the drama unfolded.

I got between the two boys. "It's alright, young men. We'll fix it." I heaved a sigh and hurried to get napkins to clean up the mess.

One of the employees noticed me cleaning the floor and came over to help out. Once we had the mess all cleaned up, Bryce looked at his vanilla cone, and the ice cream was running down the sides.

"Yuck," he murmured. "I don't want this!"

Bryce walked over and tossed his ice cream in the trashcan, then looked at me with a pleading look.

I glared at the four of them, wondering how I got talked into taking them for a day out. Then, I looked at Cody, his innocent light brown eyes, so big and loving. He was a sweet kid, and I would suffer the abuse of dealing with his friends only for him.

"I'll get you both a new chocolate cone," I said to Jason and Bryce, who seemed happy with that.

Cody smiled at me when I came back with two new chocolate cones. In his smile, he was thanking me for settling the score between his friends.

Bryce got his chocolate cone and said, "Maybe I want strawberry."

I glared at him, this time ready to give him a piece of my mind. *Should I even argue with a ten-year-old?*

He snickered. "I'm kidding…chocolate is great."

The kids happily ate their ice cream as I tried to focus on my own before it melted and got everything sticky. And this was just the beginning of the day. After the five of us finished eating, we loaded back into my car and headed to Matt's house.

"What do you guys want to do now?" I asked as we got out of the car.

"Play video games," came from Max.

"No, let's play catch," was Jason.

"Let's play Monopoly," said Bryce.

"How about we put the suggestions in a bowl and draw one out, and that's what we will do first. Deal?" I recommended.

Cody shrugged, seeming to be willing to compromise with whoever won the draw.

"Deal," they all piped in unison.

I wrote down their four suggestions. Play *War*, play football, watch a movie, and play Monopoly.

"Who wants to draw out the winner?" I asked.

"You should do it, Tasha," Cody suggested.

"Okay." I held up the jar and swished the papers around, then pulled out game number one. "Football," I announced, which was met by three groans. *Glad it wasn't War.*

We went out to the backyard, where I sat back and watched as the boys chose two separate teams. After a while, the three who didn't want to play started to get into it. I was pleased the compromise worked, at least for the first twenty minutes. Then, Bryce was running with the ball towards the goal, and Jason must've still had it out for him over the ice cream situation because Jason ran into Bryce like a freight train, tackling him to the ground and pinning him.

"Ouch!" Bryce hollered, the minute his knee made contact with the ground.

I ran to him. "Are you alright?"

Jason rolled off Bryce, looking pleased with the damage he had done. Bryce rolled onto his back and held his knee. Blood seeped through his pants.

"Bryce, let me clean your knee up," I instructed, helping him up to go inside.

Bryce leaned against me to walk into the house. We went to the bathroom, and he sat on the toilet. I pulled his pant leg up, and sure enough, he had a gash on his knee. I looked in the medicine cabinets and drawers and located antibiotic cream, gauze, and tape I could use for dressing.

"Does it hurt?" I asked, wiping it clean and putting the cream on it.

"It stings, but I'm tough," he asserted.

"I see you are." I smiled and finished taping Bryce up. "There. You're as good as new."

"Thanks!" He pulled his pant leg down, then stood up.

That was when I heard Cody. "Uh…Tasha?"

I looked to find him standing at the door, his fingers squeezing his nose as blood dripped onto his shirt.

"Cody, baby, what happened to you?"

Max followed up the rear. "Uh…I kind of hit him with the football."

Kind of? This was turning out to be a long afternoon. I wondered when it would be time to take these kids home as I helped Cody into the bathroom.

"Keep pinching the front of your nose while I go get you an ice pack," I ordered Cody.

"Okay, Tasha. Sorry for messing up my shirt."

"No, Cody, don't you apologize for anything. It was a mistake."

"I'm sorry for hitting him that hard, Miss. Tasha."

"It's not your fault either, Max. You guys hang tight here while I get an ice pack."

By the time I returned with the ice pack, the bleeding had subsided. I sent Cody to his room to change shirts and decided the rest of the afternoon they would do something with low impact and involved quietness. I put in a movie because I certainly didn't want them to play a game called *War.* It looked like they had already been through a war.

When the movie was over, I declared, "I hope you guys had a great time, but it's time that I take you home. Put your shoes on."

They groaned and begged to stay a little longer, but I couldn't do it. I was beaten and figured to regain my sanity, I needed to take the boys home. Matt would be back soon, and the cook had started preparing supper.

We got in my vehicle and rode to their respective houses. Smiling and waving as each one got out of my car, every bone in my body was tired, and I just wanted to get home and crash into my bed.

Max was the last person to get dropped off. After he got out and walked up to his door, Cody turned to me.

"Thanks so much for today, Miss Tasha. It was the best time of my life," he excitedly said.

Unsure how to respond, I got a little choked up. When we got back to Matt's place, his car was in the driveway. *Freedom is near,* I thought, ready to go home and curl up and do absolutely nothing but listen to the complete silence of my apartment.

I walked Cody to the door, opening it with my key.

"Hey, Uncle Matt, we're back?" Cody hollered out.

I wasn't moving as quickly as Cody was when Matt rounded the corner and smiled.

"Hello there. Did you have a nice afternoon?" he asked.

"It was great!" Cody said. "I got a bloody nose, and Tasha fixed it right up."

"Is that right?" Matt shot me a questioning look.

I shook my head, wondering why this kid always led with the bad news. "We might have had a few mishaps while they were playing football, but overall the day went according to plan."

Matt looked back at Cody, who was smiling from ear to ear. "Glad you had fun, my man. Run upstairs and get washed up because the food will be on the table in a minute."

"Bye, Tasha!" Cody called out as he ran up the stairs.

"Bye, buddy." I glanced at Matt as my voice drifted away. "Did you have a good day at work?"

He nodded. "Yes, it was a good day. Thanks for asking." Matt moved closer to me and, to my surprise, lifted his hand and brushed a strand of hair away from my cheek. "So, the kids didn't give you too hard of a time today, I hope." He dropped his hand slowly, still teasing me with the idea of babysitting four boys at a time.

"I managed," I stated truthfully.

"I'm impressed. I thought the drama at the ice cream parlor would have ruined the day for you." He winked at me, and at that moment, I knew he had been watching us.

"Were you spying on me today?" I asked.

"Well, I planned to help you out if you needed it while you were in the lion's den. But you patched up that one boy's knee and took care of Cody like you were a regular Florence Nightingale."

I shook my head and punched him in the shoulder. He pretended it hurt but laughed.

"You could have helped me out since you were watching everything play out, stalker uncle."

"But you said that it would be amazing, and you could handle it. I just wanted to give you the benefit of the doubt, and, honestly, I couldn't have handled it any better. You did a good job."

I blushed. "Thanks, but I'm exhausted."

That caused both of us to laugh and, at that moment, we were just two people that were no longer boss and employee. It felt like he was someone I could now call a friend.

"Sometimes, I don't even realize how I get through each day trying to raise Cody."

"You do a wonderful job. You really should know that," I said, invoking another smile to spread across his handsome face.

"Thanks, Tasha." He looked away from me, which meant something was on this mind. "You wanna stay for dinner?"

Usually, I would have taken him up on the offer. I wanted to stay but felt gross and just wanted to go home, take a shower, and rest in my pajamas.

"Thanks for offering, but I wouldn't be good company tonight. Maybe a rain check?"

"Anytime, the invitation is always open." He walked to the door and opened it.

Making the mistake of looking up into his eyes, I nearly changed my mind about dinner as I got enraptured by his magnetic aura. But, I reluctantly said, "Goodbye, Matt. I'll see you tomorrow."

"Yes, see you tomorrow, Tasha."

I strolled out of the house, feeling his eyes all over me. A smile crept upon my lips. If every encounter with him could be that sweet, then I would never want to leave. I had intentionally not allowed myself to get too attached. I didn't want to get in too deep emotionally with Matt and Cody, only to find it all gone in the blink of an eye.

Chapter Eight

Tasha

Too Hot to Handle

A week went by since I braved a day with four ten-year-olds. I was lounging around my apartment, ready for another quiet day of watching TV when my phone rang. It was Matt.

"I'm so sorry to interrupt your day. I know this is short notice," he said before explaining he needed me to come over right away to stay with Cody. "I hope you don't mind staying overnight, too. Last year when I attended this gala, I didn't get home until after three a.m. because of the long drive from Orlando to Miami. This time, I might just rent a room instead of driving back."

I looked at my TV that had Netflix queued up to play a full season of Scandal. "I don't mind, Matt," I said without giving it much thought. I had looked forward to lazing around all day doing nothing, but laying my eyes on Matt and spending time with Cody had become my addiction.

"Oh, I'm glad you can come. Cody wouldn't be comfortable with anyone other than you."

I could sense the relief in his voice.

"No problem. I'll be there within an hour."

"Thank you, and again, I'm sorry to ask you on such short notice, but I wasn't planning to go. I just got word that

Rihanna will be attending with Drake, and it will be a great networking opportunity."

"Say no more, Mr. Wilde." I had been calling him Matt. However, Mr. Wilde had seemed fitting at the moment. Now and then, I liked to remind myself that, though we were friendly toward one another, he was my boss and I was his employee.

"You're a lifesaver, Tasha. You can expect a bonus on this week's check. But there's one more thing…"

"What's that?"

"That's the last time I want to hear you call me Mr. Wilde. I feel we've been through a lot this past month, and I want to let go of the formalities. Besides, you're making me feel extremely old." I could almost hear the smile on his face as he spoke.

In the past month, we had indeed been through a lot. Starting with me nearly burning his place down to the incident with the bully and him spying on me on the boys' day out adventure.

"I'm sorry…Matt," I corrected. His name felt good rolling off my tongue. I imagined the sound of his name bouncing off the walls in the middle of hot butt naked sex. "I didn't mean to make you feel old, but I'm a few months shy of thirty myself, and I know you're not older than me." *If he is, he damn sure doesn't look it.*

"I'm close to that number," he said and laughed. "See you when you get here."

"Okay, I'll be there as soon as I can."

When I arrived, Matt offered me one of his guestrooms—a well-decorated room big enough to spread out my entire apartment in.

Cody and I hung out in the den all night playing cards and board games until we were too exhausted to hold our eyes open. I tucked him into his bed and came back downstairs. I didn't even make it to the guestroom and, instead, crashed on the couch. Sometime during the night, though, I got restless.

After tossing and turning for hours on the uncomfortable couch, I got up and walked to the bathroom on the first floor. It was next door to Matt's ground floor master bedroom. After I relieved my bladder, I washed my hands and came out of the bathroom. I headed to the guestroom; however, for an unexplainable reason, I stood at his closed door with the nagging desire to see how the room he slept in every night looked.

I shouldn't have done it, but curiosity lured me to peek inside. I turned the knob and walked into the super large room where elegance wrapped its arms around me once I stepped inside. My sock-covered feet sank into the feathered carpet as I floated over to his bed and stared at the massive mound of comfortable looking cream-colored fabrics.

Unable to control the urge, I sank into Matt's comfortable bed, feeling him all around me. Within minutes of laying my head on the pillow, darkness enveloped me, and I immediately drifted off into a cloud of dreams. Expensive cotton made a difference in my sleeping experience. I laid there floating through soft cotton clouds for hours and what seemed like days until I gasped. Matt had found me in the clouds and pulled me against his warm body. I smiled as we both started floating together. It felt so good snuggling against him that I enjoyed every minute of it, so much so, I didn't want to wake up.

Jesus, just let me take this feeling out of my dreams and with me forever, I prayed in my dream.

The moment our lips met, I arched my body against his. Shockwaves from his kiss traveled all through me. That dream had to be ranked up at the top of my best dreams ever, so good that it felt real. Too real. His tongue explored my mouth gently at first, then with an urgency that caused me to moan.

"Oh, God, please don't stop," I murmured against his lips.

"I won't stop, ever." His enthusiastic response made my eyes buck open.

I was indeed in the darkness of Matt's bedroom with very real hands clasping my cheeks and kissing me passionately. I pushed him, and he fell back on the bed with a satisfied smile spread across his face.

It wasn't a dream.

Shit, I wasn't dreaming…

I jumped away from him as if he were hot grease burning my skin. "What the hell are you doing here, Matt?"

"What do you mean? I live here."

"I know, but why were you kissing me."

"I was following your lead, Tasha."

"My lead? Oh, my God. You were in bed with me!" I yelped, still in shock that I had kissed my boss and loved every delicious morsel of it.

This wasn't supposed to happen.

"First off, you're in my bed. Second, I leaned down and was about to let you know I was here, and you kissed me." Matt smiled brightly. He wouldn't stop staring at my swollen lips that still yearned for his to devour them.

I looked around the room. He was right. "I-I- *am* in your bed." My face fell. How could I be so stupid as to fall asleep in there? "I'm sorry. It's been so nice working here, and I know that this might change things, but I didn't mean for this to happen. I was sleep, then went to the bathroom and ended up in here," the words rushed out as I stared at him blankly. I was still amazed my dream had become a reality.

"Tasha, calm down." His husky voice oozed with sex appeal.

"Am I fired again? Please don't fire me." With my luck, this would qualify as sexual harassment in the workplace on my end.

"Not on your life. After that kiss, you're hired on permanently." He chuckled.

The last thing this situation was, was funny.

"Matt, this isn't right. I shouldn't have gotten in your bed." I looked away from him because my face had to be a thousand shades of brown and maybe even a hint of red. "I'm sorry that I did...um...this." I looked at his bed and quickly scrambled out from under his covers. "Since you're home now, I'll grab my bag and leave. Goodnight!" I began making my escape, but he grabbed my hand.

"Please, don't go," he implored in a husky whisper that made my knees buckle.

I was unable to move any further away from him. I opened my mouth to tell him I didn't want to leave him, but it

68

would be best that I did, but a frantic holler sucked the words out of my mouth.

"Tasha? TASHA!" Cody's screams were enough to tear anyone's attention from what they were doing, even if it involved the potential of being seduced by a tall, gorgeous, successful man that smelled a mixture of martinis and lightly sprayed Clive Christian cologne. Matt was walking sex.

I glanced once more at him. Then, without a word, I left his bedroom, hurried up the steps to Cody's room, and heard his voice again.

"Tasha...where are you?" yelled Cody.

I entered his room, went over to his bed, and sat on the edge, pulling him towards me. "What's wrong, buddy?"

He looked at me with fear in his eyes.

"I had a bad dream," his small voice trembled out.

"I'm here now," I whispered, holding him while reciting soothing things to comfort him. "You're safe now, Cody. No one is ever going to bother you as long as I'm here."

As he was about to doze off, I heard his soft words of, "I love you."

My heart swelled.

"I love you too, little buddy."

I kissed the top of his forehead and waited for him to fall into a deep sleep before I slid him into his bed and quietly left his room.

Matt was standing close by the doorway, and his smile let me know he had been looking in on us.

"You are wonderful with him," Matt imparted.

"It's easy because he's a wonderful kid."

Matt took my hand and led me downstairs, pulling me behind him. I thought about his lips on mine. My heart was still fluttering over that kiss. I would store it in the lost files with every other dream I'd had because it couldn't happen again. When we reached the den, he began to pull me toward his room. I stopped at his door, which was still open, and fought the urge to peek inside.

Matt walked inside, then turned to me and tilted his head, quietly asking me to follow his lead. I swallowed the lump in my throat. My better judgment told me I should leave, but I stepped forward. My mouth hung open when I got a side profile of Matt standing in just a pair of Budweiser lounge pants he must've changed into when I went up to check on Cody. The cuts of his hard muscles glowed marvelously with the moonlight shining into the room.

"Tasha."

"Uh…yeah…"

"You are perfect…for Cody."

"No problem. He just had a bad dream."

He nodded and moved closer to me. "Not all dreams can be good ones," he said, hinting about my admission of how I thought kissing him was a dream.

His hand caressed my cheek. The heat from it caused me to close my eyes and relish his touch.

"Matt…I should go," I whispered.

"Why are you still thinking?" was his simple response, before he wrapped his arms around me and pulled me into a kiss.

I slipped my hand up and massaged the nape of his neck, and his tongue slipped between my opened lips. Yeah, I was no longer thinking. I needed this.

"I need this," he groaned against my lips, reaffirming the way I felt, and that was all it took for me to give in to the desire that raged deeply within me.

I hadn't slept with a man in over a year, and there Matt was, standing in front of me, sexy as hell, with longing in his eyes. Even if it was only temporary, I wanted every drop of it.

I stepped fully into his room, and he closed the door behind us. He slowly lifted my shirt up and over my head, tossing it to the floor as he walked me to his bed. He unlatched the clasp to my bra, and I slipped out of it. My breasts brushed against his naked chest, and the feeling was ecstasy.

Matt sat down on the edge of the bed, causing our lips to part. The hunger in those brown eyes as he slowly started to undo my jeans was enough to bring a tear to my eye. Matt smirked, and I couldn't stop staring at those sexy lips.

As I kicked out of my jeans, he grabbed onto my panties and pulled them down. I leaned into him, kissing him and pressing him down to the bed. He wrapped his arm around my waist and pulled me closer to him as he scooted back on the bed, so we were now flush with the mattress. I gripped onto his lounge pants and pulled them down, wiggling them down his legs until they were gone. His large hand cupped the back of my head, and we stayed in that position writhing flesh to flesh, getting acquainted with the feel of becoming one. His manhood rode alongside my leg as we melted together. I spread my legs wide, and his swelling erection rested against my opening.

Sleeping with my boss felt so wrong, yet nothing could be more right.

"Tasha, I don't have any condoms," he revealed, between kisses that heated every spot he kissed.

"I don't either."

"Are you on the pill?"

I nodded 'yes" and lowered my lips to his chest and started trailing kisses over it. Magnetism was the best way to describe the pull to him. Feeling his engorged head touching my flesh, longing for more, I craved it. There was no way I could deprive us of a meeting that felt so natural.

My lips wandered back up his chest until I sucked in his bottom lip for a kiss. I devoured his sugary sweet kisses, then positioned myself so that I was directly over his erection. I slid my tongue along his, crashing wildly against him as I guided him into me. Slipping my hand back up to his arm, I sank down onto him, fully taking him in.

"God, Tasha!" he moaned, thrusting deeper into me.

I shifted my body and just relaxed, keeping him buried inside of me as I rode him. His mouth trailed fiery kisses around my lips as my pussy tingled with a pressure that had been building inside of me. I could feel the tightness in my stomach muscles clenching as every plunge caused me to whimper and my insides to heat to a burning blaze.

My breathing increased every time we crashed against one another in his oversized bed. My hands latched onto him as I dragged my nails down his chest. I rode him smoothly, tossing my head back to focus on the feel of his hands all over me.

Matt's eyes were wide open, gaping at me, with his smile curved up in this sensual way. I lifted and lowered my body onto him, letting his dick plunge into me as I let out a scream that was sure to wake up the neighbors. I bit my lower lip to control my screams. Matt chuckled, wrapping his arm around my back and lowering me back down to him to smother my moans with equally moan-worthy fiery kisses. My pussy contracted, drawing him in as he expanded inside of me. His body grew tense, and I knew he wouldn't be able to contain his need to empty his seed into me, so I grabbed onto his shoulders and thrust harder.

"That a girl. Yes," he growled as my body shook above his.

A gasp forced me to part from the kiss. "Ahhhhh…" I cried as spasms overtook me, the bed shaking until my orgasm subsided.

With one final thrust into my heat, Matt burst through my core and shuddered. I fell on top of him, breathing heavily, my lips dropping to his shoulder. I kissed him softly, too tired to do anything else.

I started giggling, falling off him onto the bed. I couldn't control the giggles. Matt leaned over to stare at me.

"Why are you laughing?" he asked, brushing a hair behind my ear.

My breathing was raspy as I said, "That was so hot; I don't even know how to describe it."

"Hot is a pretty good word," he said, leaning in to kiss me.

I closed my eyes, feeling swoon-worthy like something from the movies. I just hoped this wasn't too hot for us to handle as boss and employee.

Chapter Nine

Matt

Waking Up

When my eyes fluttered open the next morning, I laid in bed nose to nose with my babysitter and smiled nonstop. I had been astonished by her beautiful aura the moment I laid eyes on her, and it felt incredible to know last night wasn't a dream. It had been a few years since a woman was in my bed at sunrise. Whether Tasha knew it or not, she had broken that dry spell and claimed every corner of my heart in just one night. But, she had been growing on me ever since she came strutting in here with her resume in hand.

Tasha must've sensed me staring, and her eyes opened and met mine.

"Good morning, Tasha." I gazed into her beautiful brown eyes that up close I noticed had a few specks of hazel sprinkled in her orbs.

"Were you staring at me while I was asleep? Oh my gosh." She sat straight up. "Was I snoring and woke you up? I'm sorry," she quickly apologized, then covered her mouth and giggled. Her face brightened, and a cute blush rose on her cheeks, which was the sweetest sight I had ever seen.

"Yes, I have been staring at you while you slept. It's the most beautiful sight I've seen in my life. Even your soft snoring

75

is beautiful, but that's not what woke me up," I told her as I ran the pad of my finger up and down her delicate cheek.

She grinned. "Awe, you're the first person to tell me that my snoring is beautiful. But you don't have to lie to me if I cheated you out of a night of sleep. I'll remember to use my sleeping oils next time."

My lips covered hers, breaking off her words. I gently led her back down to the bed and covered her body with mine. It was my way of saying I didn't want to hear her ramble on about snoring. However, I did appreciate her mentioning there would be a next time. If I had it my way, there would be many more nights like the one we shared. After our first explosive time making love, I woke her up many times during the night to have her again.

"You didn't wake me up, Tasha," I updated her while sucking her bottom lip into mine.

"Why are you up so early then?"

"Well, let's see. I have a super sexy woman in my bed driving me wild; I'd be a fool to spend my time with her asleep." Sleep was overrated.

"We just went to bed a few hours ago, Matt." She chuckled at her statement, and the sound of her laugh was music to my ears.

"I know, but three hours of sleep is all I need today." I studied her for a long while. Then, an idea came to me. "Hey, what are you doing this weekend?"

"I didn't have any plans. Well, other than catching up on my Netflix shows, but I guess that's not the most exciting plan, is it?"

"No, it's not," I laughed out. "We can do better than that. How about this? I've wanted to take Cody to Colorado for a ski trip for a long time, and I couldn't think of anything more perfect for us to do with the rest of the weekend than to catch a flight up there and hit the slopes. Are you down?"

"Colorado, Matt? That's a long way from Miami on short notice, and I've never been skiing before, and it's not something I'd have on my bucket list, and—I don't know." There was a softness in her stare, but I saw some heavy apprehension.

"There's nothing like stepping out of your comfort zone, babe. So, we should get out of this bed and get ready to do it," I motivated as I kissed each of her cheeks.

"But, Matt…"

"No buts! Let's get up and go."

She laughed and looked longingly into my eyes. "If you want me to get out of bed, why are you lying on top of me?"

My eyes wandered down her half-naked body, and I groaned. My cock twitched just thinking about her and the way she made me feel when we were having sex several hours earlier. "Because as much as I want you out of this bed getting dressed, I want you in it just as much."

My body was in a heated frenzy as I took all of Tasha in, her short stature lying barely naked underneath me and her small, soft hands touching my back. She only wore my T-shirt. Underneath, I knew she was still minus her panties. My thick erection rested between her thighs, and I crashed and burned when I pulled her against me for another of her soul-stirring kisses. I wanted her in my bed, pleasing me, more than I wanted to go to Colorado.

"Mmmm, Matt," she moaned as I pulled the blankets over our heads, covered her body entirely, and sank inside of her. Her whimpers and moans, along with my name screaming from her mouth, made me see stars bursting in air. I lost my good senses as I fucked Tasha for all the pleasure I denied myself over the past two years.

I didn't realize how much I craved sex until I was with her. However, it was clear to see that it wasn't just sex driving my connection to her. A lot of women had offered me sex, thrown themselves at me ready to give whatever pleasures I wanted to extract from them, babysitters included. Tasha was the one that caused me to give in. Something about her made me cave, and I didn't want to be with anyone else.

Her body reacted to mine, and she melted into me, my cock swiftly going in and out of her. I expanded with every thrust, and her hips shot against mine.

"Tasha," I whimpered, my erection plunging inside of her as her breaths increased against my neck.

Her body shifted beneath mine, and she let out soft moans that had me twisting and grinding harder against her. She tossed her head back, releasing a cry. The covers slipped away from our bodies as I came inside of her. Her body shook against mine. Her lips sought out mine, and we laid in the bed just kissing, pouring our hearts and souls from one to the other.

Chapter Ten

Tasha

Welcome to Colorado

It didn't take much convincing to get me to come to Colorado, a state that welcomes the hordes of tourists that flock in during the ski season to explore the cold weather and wild winds. Florida, this time of year, was bearable, but the snow in Colorado came down so hard it was like a thick blanket draped all around, making it hard to see anything out of our cabin window but mountains of snow. If not for the dark trees poking out from the icicles, all I would see is snow.

Matt had kissed my cold cheek before he left out to go to the sports shop, and that warmed me up a little. He asked that I be ready to hit the slopes when he and Cody returned to the cabin, so I was sitting on the sofa in the living room area when he walked back in. But ready, I was not.

Cody slipped away to his bedroom. Matt headed in my direction.

"Why am I in Breckenridge, Colorado, in the middle of winter in a cold-as-ice cabin?" I sniped as he got to me. I inhaled his scent, which made my scowl disappear as a smile graced my face.

"Tasha, if you're complaining about how cool it is in here, wait until you go outside. It's friggin' below zero out there. This city is a lot of things, but it's not warm like Miami." Matt's words were not reassuring.

I rubbed my arms through the sweater and thermal underwear I had on, shooting him a sharp glance. "No wonder I stay in the south. It's too damn cold up here. Do we have to go outside today?" I pouted as an incentive for him to agree to stay indoors, where it was a hell of a lot warmer.

Matt wasn't having any of that, and he explained why he wanted us to go out. "Tasha, baby, I'm going to have fun watching you freeze your butt off on the slopes. But not to worry, I will surely warm you up tonight," he breathed in my ear.

"No, Matt." My teeth chattered about the same time I said that. "How about we skip the freezing and just stay warm together?"

"I'll be there to keep you warm every step of the way, but we're skiing. Cody will kill me if he finds out I brought him up here to keep him cooped in this cabin."

"Well, alright, I could never let Cody down?" I acquiesced, and two hours later, I found myself trekking through the snow in knee-high snow boots.

This was bound to be a mess, I just knew it was. Matt gave me a sexy grin, and I tried to not think of all the negative things that could happen—like me falling down the mountainside and disappearing under several feet of snow, painfully freezing to death, my corpse only to be found when spring came and melted the snow.

"What are you smiling about?" I asked, raising an eyebrow.

He chuckled. "You are a cute little snow bunny." He touched my nose, and I rolled my eyes yet found it endearing all the same.

"Yeah, Tasha, you're a cute little snow bunny," repeated Cody. Matt and me both found that hilarious as we turned to Cody. He smirked, and I moved closer to him.

"I'm gonna get you." I touched his hips, tickling him until he burst into giggles. I was unable to hold that posture with my snow boots, so I wound up falling with Cody into a pile of snow. Instantly shivering, I laughed loudly. I was having the fantastic time that I didn't think I would.

I glanced at Matt. He was cracking up at the two of us lying in the snow.

"You think this is funny?" I asked.

When he laughed again, I reached up and grabbed his hand, pulling him down on top of me into the bone-chilling snow.

He only laughed harder, peering down at me. His eyes shone with happiness. He glanced at Cody, who was distracted by making a snow angel. Matt leaned in, giving me a soft peck that lived up to his promise to keep me warm. He then stood to his feet and grabbed my hand, pulling me up after him.

I fell into him, which caused us to laugh again. Then, I looked down at Cody, and he proudly was looking at his snow angel. I never felt so attached to two people in my adult life, at least not two people that weren't my blood family. Dare I call this feeling...love?

"Are you ready to head to the slopes?" Matt asked, breaking me from my thoughts.

I frowned, turning to him. "Seriously? And lose this magical moment?"

He found my teasing amusing. "Well, there's magic on the slopes too." He winked at me and took my hand in his. "We could go to the bunny slopes," he said.

The bunny slopes were for beginners, and Matt and Cody taunted me about being a novice, but I had broad shoulders. I could handle their teasing. What I wasn't about to do was pretend I could get on the advanced slopes. My priority was staying alive. Going high on a mountain to freefall to my death didn't fit that objective.

"The bunny slope would be great. I think Cody should have someone to ski with him, right buddy?" I asked.

Cody laughed. "Um...Tasha, I was planning on going on the medium slopes." He smirked. "But if you don't want to ski alone, then I suppose I can go on the bunny slopes with you for the first time."

Sheeze, I tried my best not to show it on my face, but on the inside, I was nervous. Still, if Cody could handle it, then so could I. I wasn't going to wimp out and let a ten-year-old be tougher than me. "Please...I was born for these slopes." I almost believed it.

Matt laughed. He had been doing a lot of that lately, a sharp contrast from the man who fired me on my first day working for him. "Tasha, you don't have to say that. We don't want to rush you into something you're not comfortable doing. You can take things slow, and we won't mind one bit." He winked at Cody. "Will we?"

Cody shook his head. "Not at all. We'll understand." He winked back at Matt.

Cody was talking to me like he was the grownup, and I was the kid. I wrapped my arms around him, pulling him back to me. "Just try to get me off those slopes," I challenged him.

We went towards the medium slopes. I saw several people there, and most seemed like old pros. I didn't let that worry me, but I was a little intimidated by them. We had to rent some skis. Matt showed me how to put them on. I was a fish out of water that was jumping into a frozen pond, but I was usually solid and wasn't going to let this get to me.

Letting out a slow breath while standing up, I was a little shaky and nearly toppled to the ground. Matt caught my arm. He looked at me with a worried look that silently communicated he would understand if I backed out.

"I've got this," I said, couldn't be shy in Cody's eyes, because I was always telling him to be strong and fight. This was my battle to win.

"Okay," Matt mumbled.

We carefully went over to the top of the hill, where an instructor was giving tips to those unsure of how it was done and details about the slopes we stood on. Everything sounded foreign to me. I could barely take it all in without getting dizzy, thinking about what could happen to me. For starters, I could really topple down the hill to my death.

At first, we stood back and watched a couple of other people. I peeked down the hill. It wasn't *that* high up. I took a few short breaths when it was our turn. Cody looked confident, but me, on the other hand, was a wreck. I didn't feel great as I stole another glance down the hill and considered all the possible outcomes of my taking off.

Matt kept encouraging me. "You look great, Tasha! You can do this."

After the fourth time of him *reassuring* me, I gave him a death stare, and he quieted down. I turned ahead and did just like the instructor said, swishing off, and there was no stopping me. I started screaming like a little girl as I attempted to keep my balance just like the woman directed me. Even though the actual slope seemed like it would only take a couple of minutes to maneuver, that was the longest two minutes of my life. When I finally reached the bottom of the hill, I couldn't remember how to stop and wound up falling to stop myself. I just laid there, staring up at the bright sky, glad I made it alive. When I heard the sweet sound of my name, I knew I was okay.

"Tasha, are you alright?" I looked to my right and saw Cody, seemingly concerned about me.

I nodded and laughed. "I'm fine, buddy. Just had a hard landing."

The next thing I knew, Matt had reached the bottom and was by my side, helping me up. "You sure you're alright?"

I brushed off my knees and nodded, shaking the snow off as we all laughed. "I'm fine."

"Falling is all a part of learning the slopes. I don't know anyone who has come out here and hasn't fallen at one point. The best part about it is the more you do it, the better you get at it, and before you know anything, you'll be half as good as I am," Matt bragged.

"Gee, thanks," I said and giggled. "I'll be sure to keep that in mind as my bones begin to crack once I thaw out." As hard as I fell, I was still having the time of my life, and it was the best feeling to be experiencing it with Matt and Cody.

***

Later that evening, I shuddered in front of the fireplace and asked Matt, "What's Cody doing?"

"He's taking a nice, long, hot bath," Matt answered and looked at me with concern in his eyes. "Would you like for me to run you one, too? You look like you could use a relaxing, steamy bath."

"Maybe later. Right now, this fire is way too inviting to get up and move from this spot. I may start freezing again if I move from in front of it."

Matt's laughter came out to play again at my expense. "Yeah...I know what you mean." He leaned back into the couch and glanced at me. "You overcame your fears out there today. You're the strongest woman I know."

"Well, I'm not all that strong, but thanks."

Matt reached out and touched my hand as our eyes met. "So, tell me something about yourself that I don't know."

We had been talking since I started working for him and definitely when things started heating up with us. "What do you want to know?"

His brow raised while he seemed to ponder that. "When you came to the house looking for a job and gave your resume, I noticed it said that you were a writer at *Colorful Times* magazine. What happened to make you leave there?"

I took in a deep breath, wanting to forget he ever asked the question.

He caught on to my angst and said, "If you don't want to tell me, you don't have to. I just figured that being a babysitter was a lot different than being a writer."

I nodded slightly. "It is, but there's not a lot to tell about *Colorful Times*. I tried to block that part of my memory from my mind."

"Oh, so what happened there that makes you want to block it out?"

The lawyer in Matt wouldn't let me get away with keeping that part of my life away from him. He was so comforting and easy to talk to that I didn't feel I needed to shy away from the truth with him either, so I let it out. "Well, it all started when I wrote this piece for the magazine." I heaved a sigh before I continued. "It was a great piece, the best I've ever written, and everyone thought so, including my boss, Melinda Lory." My left eye began twitching when I said her name, and I noticed a shift in Matt's attitude, as well. I could sense he knew the name, which wouldn't be a surprise since he was a celebrity lawyer. Everyone knew Loudmouth Melinda. "She thought it was such a great piece that she decided to promote Nina after Nina tweaked the story and turned it in as her own."

Matt's jaw dropped, and for a few seconds, he just sat there with his mouth open in shock.

"Yeah," I said faintly.

"So, she stole the article from you and passed it off as her own?"

I nodded. The pit in my stomach was still just as hollow as the day it happened. "Melinda fired me because my column was losing viewership. I had lower views because Nina stole my ideas before I could get them to print. But still, Melinda promoted Nina knowing she was stealing my work, and they fired me after using me up. That's the way my writing career goes. The End."

"That's bullshit, Tasha!" His angry roar startled me. "As a lawyer, I can assure you everything that went down with Melinda at *Colorful Times* is unlawful. You do realize that you could sue their ass for wrongful termination and copyright infringement, right?"

I had to admit the thought crossed my mind a time or two. What they did to me wasn't legal, by any means. I could prove the stories were mine, but I didn't want to put the energy into it. Besides, I had licked my wounds, healed, and was happy. No, I wasn't making the pay I was used to, but happiness wasn't always about money.

"I'm not interested in suing anyone, at least not now."

He groaned. "Tasha, if you sue, you could own the dag-on company. Then, you would be their boss."

"That's not me. I want to put it behind me. Maybe how I feel will change in the future, but for now…I'm at peace."

He looked like he wanted to object, but Cody's voice came from the bathroom. "Uncle Matt?"

"Matt, go take care of what needs taken care of with Cody. I'm okay with this decision I've made, but thanks for your concern." I pulled the blanket in my lap up over my shoulders, endeavoring to relax.

He looked like he wanted to say more, but I encouraged him not to with an assuring smile.

"Alright, I'll drop it, but anytime you're ready to take back what belongs to you, I'm here for you, baby." Matt got up from the couch and headed back to where Cody was.

"Achoo," I sneezed, then I stared at the fire as thoughts of suing Melinda and *Colorful Times* flooded my mind. There was no point in it when my life was perfect. I didn't need them, and I didn't need their money. I would be just fine. That I knew for sure. "Achoo!" Well, I'd be fine if I could get and stay warm.

Chapter Eleven

Matt

Feverish

It came on so suddenly. One minute we were discussing how she could sue her former employer, then I left to take care of Cody, and when I came back...she wasn't feeling well. She was the prettiest thing God ever put on this earth, so I couldn't fight the desire to pull her into my arms and tell her everything would be okay as she sneezed continuously. Wrapping my arms around her, I hugged her tight. I could feel her trembling. Pressing my lips to her head, I breathed in her fresh vanilla scent, but she pulled away all too soon, and I was left feeling empty.

"Matt, I'm coming down with something, and I don't want to get you sick."

I didn't care about that. I just wanted to make her comfortable.

"I'll be fine," I whispered. "Just rest against my shoulder."

We laid there, getting lost in staring at the fireplace as her soft breathing echoed in the room. I just wanted to be close to her, in sickness and health, as wedding vows would say. Yes, wedding vows passed through my mind uninvited, and it had everything to do with Tasha being the dynamic woman she was. I didn't have to force myself to think about marrying her;

it was a yearning coming from deep inside of me. That had never occurred for any other woman in my life. This was love. No ifs, ands, or buts about it.

While I dealt with that revelation, Cody had one of his own. "Uncle Matt, I'm ready for bed!"

I looked up to find him standing under the arch.

"Is she alright?" he asked, fear echoing in his voice. Cody loved her, almost as much as I did. *Yes, I love Tasha Baker.*

I nodded. "She's just coming down with something, probably from the chill in the air. She'll be fine, buddy." I slowly pulled my arm out from under her. She moaned, and her eyes fluttered open. "Tasha baby, get dressed for bed, and I'll make you some soup." I was sure we had something in the kitchen that would do.

"Thank you!" Her feeble voice was enough to break my heart. I helped her to her feet and guided her into our cabin bedroom, then went into Cody's room.

"You don't have to tuck me in, Uncle Matt. I'm ten years old."

"I know, buddy, but I like the time we spend together at the end of the day. How about you?"

Cody pulled the covers back and got underneath them. "I like it too, but Tasha could really use you to help her get well. I don't like that she's sick."

"You're a smart young man," I stated, thinking that I must've been doing something right. "Whatever would I do without you?"

Cody smiled. "I feel the same about you, Uncle Matt. I say that to myself all the time." It was a sweet moment between the two of us and one I hated to depart.

"Goodnight, buddy." I leaned down and kissed his forehead. I never thought I would be such a pushover when it came to my nephew moving in with me. I was pretty much a sucker every time he smiled at me, and especially when he looked sad. I would give anything to have my sister back in my life, but I was super blessed to have Cody, the best parts of her, there with me. The loss and gain had instantly made me a better man. He only had me to show him how to conduct himself. "See you in the morning," I bade as I walked to the door.

"Goodnight!" Cody rolled onto his side and closed his eyes.

I watched him for a minute, then left his room and went to the kitchen nook. I dug through some cabinets until I found a can of chicken noodle soup. As I thought about life without Tasha, I felt loneliness creep inside of me. There had never been such a pull toward one woman for me. With everything in me, I knew my budding love for her was real. The thought of her hurting was something I couldn't handle.

I finished cooking the soup and dished it into a bowl, then grabbed a bottle of water and headed off to our room. Tasha was under the covers with her eyes closed until I reached the bed. Then, she opened her eyes and stared up at me. She looked weak but beautiful.

"Soup's here," I stated.

She pulled herself up in bed and leaned back against the wall. I sat on the edge of the bed and dipped the spoon out to feed her. Grinning, she took a bite from my offered spoon. "I'm not that helpless. I can feed myself."

I shrugged. "I like doing things for you." I gave her another spoonful of the soup, and she took it like a good patient.

"Thank you," she uttered.

"I feel like it's the least I can do. After all, I forced you out into the cold."

She smirked. "Well, you didn't force me. I went on my own, and honestly, it was worth it. Had it not been for your insistence, I would have never gotten on the slopes," she got out before another sneeze that looked like it took the wind out of her. She pulled the cover over her legs, and I continued to feed her soup.

When she grabbed the water and opened it up to take a drink, I put the bowl down. "I'm going to get dressed for bed, so I can cuddle up with you and keep you warm."

She smiled and watched me go to the suitcase and pull out my lounge pants. Dressing in front of her, I was well aware that she was watching my every move. When I pulled my lounge pants up, I glanced at her, and she snickered.

"I will never get tired of the sight."

Even when she wasn't feeling her best, she made me smile. Walking over to the bed, I touched my lips to her heated forehead.

"I will never get tired of looking at you either, baby," I mumbled against her head.

When she looked up at me, I moved closer, slowly moving my lips to hers. As our lips connected, she tried to pull back.

"Stupid move, Matt. I can't let you get sick," she murmured.

"Oh, but it'll be worth every sneeze." I chuckled.

She gently pushed me away.

A cold could never keep me from connecting with her. "I'll worry about my health later, baby. Right now, I want to take care of you in every way, and right now, you definitely need a reason to feel good."

Without waiting on her response, I fell against her, my knee landing on the bed as I melded into her. She dropped the bottle of water on the floor. We didn't move to see if anything spilled out. Instead, I wrapped my hand around her neck, deepening the kiss I was stealing from her sweet lips.

"Matt," she breathlessly whispered against my mouth.

Her labored breathing told me she needed to rest, but there was no stopping me once I started making love to her. I forced my hand into the soft fabric of her gown and grabbed one of her breasts. She moaned at first contact. Her head leaned backward, so I had to press my body against hers to reach her ear to speak. I wanted her to hear me loud and clear.

"I'm in love with you," I said with one hand around her waist and the other still massaging her breast. I lowered my hand around her and grabbed onto her bottom, pulling her closer to my rising cock.

"I feel the same thing for you, Matt." The urgency in her voice was heartfelt and real. There was no questioning whether she just said it because I said it first. "I want you so bad," she moaned. Her eyes darkened as if the heat flowing between us was changing their color.

I rolled over on my back, pulling her on top of me. My hand landed on her bare ass. I couldn't believe she was already ready for me, panty-free. I clutched her ass in my palm, squeezing it tightly. My arousal was at its full length when Tasha pulled back to look into my eyes. Her plump lips begged to be kissed again and again.

Madly in love with this beautiful dark angel, I would never fully understand the power she had over me. Our eyes met with smoldering heat, and I growled just before our lips met once again. Pulling her gown over her head, I exposed the ripe breasts I massaged earlier. I squeezed her soft ass cheeks into my greedy hands, grateful she was all mine to devour.

"Make love to me, Matt," she moaned raspily, suddenly not worried about getting me sick, and I was happy to oblige.

I slipped out of my PJ pants, and my hard cock sprung forward to freedom. Sliding my fingers into her hot, dripping wet slit, I growled. I had to taste her. I stuck my soaking wet fingers into my mouth and licked her sugary sweetness.

"You taste *good*, baby," I said, grinning.

I grabbed onto her legs and spread them wide. Her pussy was like a breath of fresh air, wonderful and amazing. My cock throbbed at the need to be inside of her. Positioned at her core, I plunged inside of her balls deep. She moaned out her pleasure, grabbing onto my arms as I fell into her again. My dick was on fire from the first stroke, and her jiggling ass set me ablaze each time I connected with her steaming hot pussy. Captivated by becoming one with her, I wanted more of it, and I wanted it forever. Without warning, a surge of electricity shot through to my shaft. I threw my head back into the pillow and reveled in the feel of her riding my pulsating cock. She rocked her hips harder and harder against mine, connecting us to a higher bond as I held onto her waist and thrust all the way into her. Tasha's moans drew my eyes back to her smoldering ones. I wanted to capture that look of pure desire and keep it in my memories forever.

"Fuck!" I growled as I embedded myself into her as deep as I could travel.

She collapsed against me, looking exhausted and yet full of desire for more. Her lips sunk to mine, and while I rocked back and forth underneath her, our tongues wildly danced together. Her moans of pleasure let me know the fiery heat I felt was assaulting every inch of her body too.

When we broke from the syrupy sweet kiss, it was because she was starting to seize above me, gripping my shaft tightly in between her walls, jerking uncontrollably with her mouth agape, and eyes rolling to the back of her head. She screamed out in pure ecstasy, before collapsing against me in a fit of sweat.

"Oh, God…" Tasha whimpered, and seconds later, my seed filled her as she rippled with her own orgasm.

As Tasha lay on top of me with the afterglow of lovemaking bouncing off her skin, I knew one thing was certain. We were in love, and I wanted it to last forever.

Chapter Twelve

Tasha

Party Invitation

"Come home with us," Matt tempted me once we were back in Miami.

I wanted nothing more than to spend more time with him, but I had things I needed to take care of at my apartment.

I thought of how long it had been since I'd been home. "I wish I could," I replied softly. "I have to water my plants, check my mail, and make sure all is well at my place. It's been a while."

He groaned. "I guess I can let you off work for a short while. Cody and I will survive until we see you later," Matt yielded as we pulled up to my apartment.

"Well, thank you, boss," I mocked.

"Oh, I love it when you say that," he said close to my ear.

I bit down on my lip and winked at him, then glanced toward the backseat. We tried not to flaunt our affection in Cody's face, but the kid wasn't easy to pull one over on. I was sure he knew Matt and I were dating. I leaned in and pecked Matt's cheek before turning to Cody.

"See you guys later."

"Can I at least get your bag for you?" Matt asked, looking like a sick puppy.

"No, I have it, but thanks for taking care of me when I was sick last night. I feel brand new today." The broad smile I wore was proof of that.

"Baby, I will always take care of you," Matt promised.

Cody giggled.

"Thank you, and I'll talk to you soon." I hopped out of the car with my overnight bag to trek up to my apartment.

Barely inside, my phone signaled a text message.

It was Dana.

Dana: Hey girlie. It's been a while. Meet me at El Havana in twenty minutes. I won't take no for an answer. :)

I smiled at the message. I looked around at my plants and mail and decided to take care of them later.

Me: On my way!

Without even sitting down, I grabbed my keys and headed out of my apartment. When I got to the restaurant, Dana was sitting at our table. She stood when she saw me.

"Hey, love!" she said, hugging me as I got to the table.

"Hey!" We were at our favorite Cuban restaurant, and I was so glad to be hanging out with my girl, once again.

I looked at the menu, though we both knew what we wanted and placed our order as soon as the waitress got there. When she left, Dana started in.

"How've you been? It's been so long since we talked. I'm assuming you still work with the Wilde family." She took a drink from her wine and looked at me with a side-eye.

"Oh yes…I'm still working there, and things are…well, they are going great, actually." I left it vague, not sure what I wanted to say about my relationship with Matt. "Yeah, still working there. Cody is great," I reiterated.

Dana smiled. "I'm glad to hear that, but you haven't said anything about Cody's uncle. What do you think about him?"

My soul lit up at the mention of Matt. I had to hide my blush from my friend. She knew me almost as good as I knew myself. "Oh well...he's nice." I looked off toward the doorway as if I were expecting someone.

"Nice, huh?" Dana laughed. "Girl come on...he's better than nice. He's fine, built, and has a nice ass too." She smiled and gave me a high five.

I chuckled and shrugged. "Really? Haven't noticed."

We shared a laugh that took the pressure off of me. Thankfully, Dana let it go and started discussing what was happening with her virtual assistant clients.

Our food came. We ate and finished off our wine, all the while talking about anything but Matt and Cody. I figured I had escaped having to discuss my present employer/lover. However, when we got done eating and were sitting there, Dana brought the subject up again.

"So, I'm guessing that you're watching Cody tonight while Matt goes to his party."

I frowned. He hadn't mentioned a party to me, and we talked about quite a lot over the past few days.

"Party?" I asked, trying to remain calm about it.

"Yeah. There's a celebrity couples' party for charity going on tonight. Everybody who's anybody will be there in rented clothes and expensive jewels," she laughed. "It's no kids allowed, so I just assumed Matt would've mentioned it to you so that someone could stay with Cody. It's on his schedule of events for today, and he's confirmed as attending. I checked it before I met you here." Dana took a sip from her wine glass, not realizing the thoughts running through my mind. "But maybe he's leaving Cody with a friend or something," she added more fuel to the heap of fire already burning.

Not only hadn't Matt mentioned a party to me, but he also said nothing about needing a babysitter. My face had to be a mask of confusion at a time when I needed to be discreet so that Dana wouldn't see my internal turmoil.

"Um...no...he hadn't mentioned it. Maybe he's getting someone else," I mumbled.

"Oh. That's interesting because he's funny about who he allows around Cody. From what I get about him, he's very overprotective. He doesn't have any close family in Miami, and he didn't ask me to run a background check on anyone else, so I don't know," Dana replied. She had no idea how interesting this bit of information indeed was.

"Does everyone bring a date to those types of parties?" I casually asked since Matt hadn't asked me to accompany him.

"Well yeah...most people don't like to go stag to these things. Everyone is trying to show off their status, including who's on their arm. That's fake Hollywood for you." She dry-laughed at that. "But anyway, I know Matt's bringing a date. He verified his two tickets today."

My face fell at the mere thought that Matt was taking someone else. We had been getting along so well. I didn't think he would do this to me, but it was a slap in the face. I was good enough to fuck, but not good enough to go to these bougie ass parties?

"Oh, …okay. Well, that's nice." Attempting to be blasé about this new information, I looked down at my wine glass. I didn't notice Dana staring at me until she started her nervous laughter. "What?" I asked, not amused.

"Wow…you like him, don't you?"

"What? No!" I protested, maybe too much. "I didn't know he was seeing someone. That's all."

Dana shrugged. "Doesn't mean he's seeing someone. It's a huge deal, and he would look bad not having a date."

But why am I not that date?

"I think your face is telling me that you do like him and believe me…I can't blame you. He's fine in all the right places." She wiggled her flawlessly arched eyebrows, and I looked away from her. I just needed to make sure I wasn't thinking negative things about him when he deserved better.

"Are you sure he's taking someone?"

Dana heaved a sigh. "I'll look to make sure I read it right." She grabbed her phone, pulled up his schedule, and nodded. "Yep, it says he ordered two tickets to the gala tonight." She hesitated and gave me a somber look. "I'm sorry, Tasha."

I laughed, blowing it off. "No reason to be sorry. It's not like I'm his woman or anything. I feel nothing for him. I just wish I could make that extra money babysitting." I wished I wasn't lying too. The way I felt this very moment was the reason I didn't want to get involved with my boss.

I finished off the dinner feeling like a fool as I tried desperately to keep Dana from connecting the dots to my fling with Matt. She was my best friend, so it was a good possibility she already knew my true feelings but was sparing me the embarrassment of addressing them right then.

I thought Matt genuinely liked me, but if he was putting another woman on his arm in public, then he didn't want to be seen with me. He didn't even want me to watch Cody while he went to the party, so clearly, he was hiding this from me.

Maybe he just asked me to come home with him as a ploy, knowing he would eventually take me back to my apartment, and I wouldn't suspect anything when I didn't talk to him later tonight.

Obviously, I was wrong about us. I just wondered why he was trying so hard to impress me if I was just some convenient booty.

***

I laid on the couch to watch TV later that evening, still upset that Matt was going to go out with some other woman when I heard a knock on the door.

"Coming!" I called, trudging my way to the door. When I opened it, I found a delivery man standing there with flowers and an envelope. "Hello."

"Are you Ms. Baker?" he asked.

"Yes," I confirmed, nodding my head and staring at the beautiful red roses in his hand.

"These are for you!" He handed me the flowers and envelope.

I signed the paper and thanked him, then opened the card as I shut the door behind him.

The card read:

Baby, I wanted you to come home with me so I could surprise you with a night out being treated like a queen. My queen. With this big celebrity couples party happening in a few hours, you don't have time to turn me down again. I need a date tonight, and I need it to be you. So, put on the black dress you picked out in Colorado. I'd love to see you in it again. See you at eight. Matt

Staring at the card and his writing, I couldn't believe it. There I was wallowing in self-pity, thinking he was only using me, and he wanted me to go with him all along. First, I felt guilty for even considering he would mistreat me like that. Then, I smiled and immediately jumped to getting dressed and ready for my date!

Chapter Thirteen

Matt

Dance the Night Away

The slow song came on as the DJ finished up his sentence. Tony Braxton's "Breathe Again" made me grin like a Cheshire cat as I cast my eyes toward the door. Tasha should've been there any minute. It had only been a few hours since I last saw her, but I longed for the moment to see her again. I was looking forward to showing her off as my woman. When I got the invitation, stating *plus one,* I knew she would take that spot next to me. Showing her off to the world had quickly become my obsession, and I couldn't wait for our debut as a couple. My days of attending these galas alone, or with a random pick from my address book, were officially over.

It was after nine, and I looked around the room. There was still no sign of Tasha, but plenty of celebrities, men and women who would gladly give their money for the kids, mixed and mingled and seemingly enjoyed themselves. This gala was all about pulling people together to make a difference. It also just happened to be my favorite charity.

The slow love ballad playing could have become *our* song, but since Tasha wasn't there yet, I wasn't sure we would get the chance to claim the dance floor. When my eyes made their way back to the door, I saw her. Not Tasha, but Melinda

Lory came strutting through the door. Her eyes scanned the room, and it was like a magnet drew her to me as she glanced in my direction. She beamed as a smile crossed her face. Before I could make a getaway, she headed my way.

"Hey, Matt." Her heavy makeup made her look almost clownish, and given the way she treated my lady, she looked twice as bad to me.

I nodded and spoke to her, "Hey, Melinda." Then, I turned away from her to watch the door, checking to see if Tasha would come in. The last thing I wanted was for her to find me in the vicinity of the one person she despised most.

"Beautiful night to save babies' lives, don't ya' think?" Melinda's voice grated my nerves.

I shot her a sharp look and arched an eyebrow. "Well, I would say every night is beautiful if you could save a child's life."

My tone was not inviting for further conversation, but she didn't get the hint. She cackled like the witch she was and nodded. "Well, you have me there, Matt." She then started to laugh some more while holding her hand to her chest like I was hilarious. She was being overly friendly. She reached out and touched my shoulder, stopped laughing, and caught my stare. "I never knew how strong your biceps were, Matt. Wow, you are built." She proceeded to giggle. Her eyes traveled down the cut of my tailored suit from my chest to my shoes, then back up.

"Ha." I looked away from her. It wasn't very subtle the way she was flirting, but I found it funny since I had no mutual interest in her. "Thanks, Melinda." I snickered and continued to look off in the direction of where Tasha should be entering any moment when I heard Melinda's voice again.

"I just love this song!" I turned to look at her, and she had a dreamy look in her eyes. "It's a great song to dance to, don't ya' think?" She wriggled her brows suggestively.

"Yeah, I guess so." I shouldn't have given in to her blatant plea for attention, but I was looking out of sorts just standing there anyway. She started swaying to the music in front of me, so against my better judgment, I moved slightly from side to side, swaying to the beat.

Her eyes widened with child-like glee, and I hated the clear expression of excitement on her face. "Of course, I'd love to dance with you, Matt," she said as if I had asked her a question. I hadn't.

Holding her hand out to me, she took a few steps toward the dance floor. I didn't take her hand, but I followed her, and she started to move. I maintained the perfect viewing area of the main entrance, waiting for Tasha. Melinda was talking away, and my eyes never left that location.

"We Are Family" by Sister Sledge reverberated through the room, and I swayed to the beat a little bit faster. Wrestling with whether to bring up the situation with Tasha at Melinda's magazine company, I didn't want to upset Tasha, but I also didn't want to stand by and do nothing. I could eat *Colorful Times* for dinner and spit the bones out to snack on later. The only reason I agreed to dance with Melinda was to tell her this well-known fact.

"Are you even listening to me?" Melinda asked me at one point, a sound of irritation thick in her voice. She didn't know how close I was to owning her, and not in the way she wanted me to.

"What?" I looked back at her and pretended to be surprised she would ask such a question. "Of course, I'm listening."

"Well, …you looked like you were ignoring me." Her heavily-made up face returned to looking content again.

My whole mood shifted, and a glowing smile brightened my face. Alas, I spotted Tasha stepping into the ballroom. I stopped my robotic movements, leaving Melinda swaying to the beat alone. She had no idea that she was saved by Tasha, who was breathtakingly beautiful in her black cocktail dress and a matching shawl that hung over her brown shoulders that looked almost bronze in the party's dim lighting. She was even more beautiful in that dress than when she tried it on in Colorado. I ignored the way Melinda stared at me, mouth gaping, as I gawked at the only woman who deserved my attention.

Without a word, I moved on. Tasha's eyes went to mine, and she grinned. I met her in the middle of the room, wrapped my arm around her waist, and pulled her close to me.

"You look gorgeous tonight."

She smiled with pride. "You aren't looking bad yourself, Mr. Wilde." She winked, and my lips dipped down to hers. All eyes were on us. She *was* the most beautiful woman in the room. When we parted from the kiss, she licked her lips. Seeing her tongue glide across her cherry-colored lips caused a reaction in me, one that would help me lose the battle of not walking around this party with a blatant erection.

"You're going to regret doing that, if you keep it up."

"What did I do?" she coyly asked with a raised brow. "Oh, if it's because I'm so late, I'm sorry. I appreciate the invitation, but I got it on short notice, and traffic was not on my side."

I shrugged. It didn't matter that she was late. However, I was thoroughly bothered that she had arrived looking sexier than I ever imagined. Anxious for this party to be over, I wanted to take her home and punish her with a night of pleasure for a few reasons. Being so beautiful was only one of them.

"You're the only one I want by my side, so it doesn't matter about the time as long as you're here. I was talking about you calling me Mr. Wilde."

"Oh," she giggled. "Sorry, Matt."

"Want to dance?"

She smiled and grabbed onto my extended hand. "It would be my pleasure."

I walked her out to the middle of the dance floor. From the corner of my eye, I spotted Melinda glaring at me. Tasha seemed to notice it too. Ignoring our audience of one, I wrapped my arms around Tasha, fell into a gentle beat, and swayed to "Smash Into You" by Beyoncé.

"We have an audience," she whispered a few songs later.

Melinda was still watching us and making ugly faces, which wasn't hard for her to do with her unpleasant attitude. I wasn't attracted to Melinda in the way she was drawn to me. Tasha had my heart. No other woman could change that.

"Yes, she's been on me since she got here. I don't care if she dies a slow death due to envy; the woman who has my heart is in my arms, and that's all that matters." I grazed my lips across Tasha's. "But since she's watching...we could give her something to watch."

Wrapping my hand around Tasha's neck, I pulled her into a deep kiss. When our kiss collided and danced to the beat of the contemporary ballad, I swore I heard a collective sigh coming from Melinda's direction. I wasn't about to let her ruin our night, especially when I had plans that would only make Tasha and I grow stronger.

After hours of mingling with other guests, dancing, and cuddling with Tasha, I left her side only to go to the restroom. When I returned, I walked up to Tasha and turned her around so that her back was against my body.

"Having fun?" I spoke softly in her ear.

She looked back at me and chuckled lightly. "For the most part, yes."

I frowned. "For the most part?"

She rolled her eyes. "I heard Nina and Melinda cackling over there when you left. I'm pretty sure I heard my name thrown around." She motioned with her head towards a corner where a taller, slender woman had joined Melinda. I figured she was Nina, Melinda's plus one. Neither lady had shown up with a man as their date. "A curveball was thrown her way when she spotted us together. Poor girl...I almost feel sorry for her. Almost!" Tasha said, laughing.

I glanced their way again. Nina and Melinda were staring right at us, then glancing at Tasha and breaking out laughing. Whatever they were discussing, I wasn't about to let it spoil Tasha's mood. She was enjoying the night, and they were just catty and wanting to make Tasha uncomfortable like she didn't belong at the party...or by my side.

"Baby, forget about them. Tonight is only about us. You know that, right?"

"Matt, I know that." Still, she seemed to search my eyes for something that was hard for her to find.

The two jealous women were getting to her, and I couldn't have that. Not giving her a chance to deny me, I grabbed her hand and pulled her along behind me.

"Where are we going?" she asked.

"Come with me, Tasha. I have something to show you." I quickly moved towards the outside balcony.

She could barely keep up but repeated her question. "Matt...where are we going?"

I tugged her out onto the balcony and was relieved no one else was out there. The fresh air felt good.

"Matt...what—"

"I have to show you what matters." I wrapped my arm around Tasha's waist and walked her to the side of the building then pressed her back against the wall. Standing outside of the room filled with who's who of entertainment, our lips met, and soon we were devouring each other's mouths heatedly. As my tongue grazed against hers, I pulled her leg up and around my waist, inching her dress up so that I could touch between her legs. I stroked her inner thighs, and she jerked against me, just from the feel of my hand on her skin.

She laughed as I tickled her slightly. "Matt...they can see us," she breathlessly spoke, parting from the kiss and pointing toward the door we exited.

"Who cares? I'm showing you who this night is about right now… us."

Her eyes lifted to mine, and she had a naughty grin on her lips. I cradled her neck in my hands, towing her to me and bringing her lips back to mine. Tasha gasped, tossing her head back against the building.

"You'll care when we get arrested for indecent exposure," she said, giggling sweetly then pushed me away and took a step toward the door, but it was too late. I had to have her.

She looked like she was about to argue when I pulled her back to me and captured her lips once more. But a moan resonated from her, and she trailed her fingers along the back of my neck, getting lost in the moment.

Taking her hand, I pulled her further away from the slide door, to the balcony's furthest corner. Tasha giggled when I turned her around so that her back was to me, and I was facing her dress zipper.

"Matt, we can't…"

"Oh, yes, we can, and we will." I lifted her hair up and out of the way and slowly slid the zipper down. Removing one shoulder from the dress, I took my lips to her shoulder. She murmured something about us getting caught, but I ignored her and planted my bulging erection at the center of her ass, swaying my hips to our beat.

She tossed her head back and stared up at the sky. I imagined she was praying we didn't get caught, as I slowly dragged her dress up.

"Matt…" her voice trailed away with the cold winter air that seemed to pick up in intensity, causing me to move faster to get her dress over her ass so that I could heat us both.

She turned to me, looking at the zipper of my pants with a sneaky grin. She took over, grabbed onto the zipper, and pulled it down teasingly slow. I looped my fingers into the sides of her panties and tugged them down as well. She grabbed onto my boxers and pulled them down enough to release my manhood. With my cock exposed and her heated wetness ready for me, I pushed her back against the building and hungrily kissed her. My tongue slipped between her lips and collided with her sweet tongue.

"I can't believe we're doing this," she murmured between kisses.

"Oh, baby," I growled against her lips when she reached down and started to stroke my erection, making me rock hard. "We're just getting started," I said and excitedly rammed my tongue in and out of her mouth. I groped her soft and succulent breasts and moaned into her ear. The aching in my cock had me longing to be buried inside of her. The tip touched her opening, and her wetness was spilling over, driving me insane just from the slickness of her juices in contact with my dick.

She lifted her hand that was touching my dick and placed it on my arm, and I pressed myself against her. My lips left hers, and I went down and started to kiss her neck. Then, I swiftly lifted her right leg and plunged into her sweet abyss. She whimpered, and I withdrew my erection and plowed back into her.

"Yes…oh God Matt…yes…" she moaned.

Her eager acceptance of me gave me extra energy. I pulled back and out of her, then rammed into her again, bucking my hips against her fast and hard. She shrieked, and my fluid and quick thrusts continued with the aim of taking us both to ecstasy. She bucked her hips harder and harder against me until we settled into a motion of pure desire raging through us.

My erection expanded in her warm pussy. She bit down on my shoulder to keep from screaming and blowing our cover to all the guests of the party. The sharp pain that shot through my shoulder wasn't anything I couldn't deal with as I pounded in and out of her while rubbing my hands up and down her back, massaging her with pleasure.

I tried not to focus on my breathing, but I could see my breath in the cold air as I exhaled deeply.

"Tasha, I love you so much," I groaned out against her ear.

"I love you too, Matt," she said and spread her legs open wider, giving me the ample room I desired to have her without any constraints.

When she let out a pulsating squeal, my cum gushed into her, emptying all the life that shot forth into her precious tunnel. Her gushing hot liquid wrapped around my erection, causing me to collapse against her due to unimaginable delight. I pushed her harder against the wall, and our lips collided as I slid in and out of her, still releasing until I heard rustling behind us. I jerked out of her, and her eyes got big.

She quickly fixed her dress and panties as I gathered my pants around my waist, and then she turned around so that I could help her out with her zipper. As I slid up her zipper, she looked ahead. I could hear her heart beating from the rush. A couple walked out on the balcony, and I zipped up my pants, just as they turned to look at us. I smiled and nodded in their direction, and Tasha glanced at me. She had the widest grin on her face, almost giving us up with her guilty-looking eyes.

I smiled at her and grabbed her hand. "Shall we?" I asked, winking at her.

She turned toward the entrance. "Sure, thanks for showing me the stars, Matt," she said, and we held hands as we bypassed the couple and headed back to the party.

We each held a sneaky grin as we narrowly escaped getting caught. Once inside, Tasha looked up at me, and we erupted into laughter. We needed that time to feel each other so that we could relax. I pulled Tasha closer to me as we walked further into the ballroom. The party was still in full swing, but I couldn't wait to get her home. If Melinda knew how sprung I was over Tasha, her head would explode.

Chapter Fourteen

Tasha

The Next Step

"Tonight was…fun," I voiced after Matt escorted me to my door.

"What was your favorite part?"

"Hmmm…well, I'm sure it wasn't you dancing with Melinda."

He took a step back. "Ouch! About that… I was only dancing with her because—"

"Matt, I know you don't like her like that. I hope you didn't confront her about firing me."

He looked relieved that I wasn't really upset with him about dancing with Melinda. "I didn't bring it up tonight," he assured me.

"You are hilarious, though. You should have seen your face just now." I grabbed onto his suit jacket and pulled him to me. "I would have to say sex on the balcony was the highlight of the night." My voice was husky as my lips covered his for another sanctimonious dance.

As the kiss momentarily broke, he agreed, "The balcony scene was priceless." His lips immediately latched back onto mine.

"Who's watching Cody?" I asked, between his sprinkle of sensual kisses.

114

"He's staying overnight with a friend."

"Oh?" I pulled him into my apartment since it was apparent this would not be our goodnight kiss.

The moment the door closed, we started to undress one another frantically. Discarded clothing led a path back to my bedroom, and once we were there, the only thing left was to slip off my bra, which I did with ease. I pushed Matt down to the bed, and he looked up at me. His breathing already labored. I got on the bed, planting my knees to either side of him, and ran my hands down his chest. I lowered myself to his chest, where I started kissing and nibbling lightly along his breast line. He growled, and my eyes went to his.

He had this silly grin on his face that said he didn't want to take it slow, but I had him right where I wanted him. I plucked my teeth around his nipple, and he slipped his hands up my back, sighing with pleasure as he pressed his palms deep into my skin.

When I swirled my tongue around his nipple, he elicited a deep moan. I softly trailed my lips down his stomach, inching myself closer to his erection. That's when I slowly flicked my tongue, running it around his engorged head.

"God, Tasha..." he moaned and squirmed beneath me.

Licking his tip, I smiled deviously. Matt rewarded my efforts with an exasperated grunt, so I ran my tongue from the base to the tip of his manhood then playfully along the other side.

"Shit!" he muttered in a strained voice.

I giggled, moving back up to his lips and leaving his erection close to climax. Grinning as I looked down at the fully-pleasured look gracing his handsome features. "What's wrong, babe?" I asked.

He shook his head, bit down on his bottom lip, and let me know in no uncertain terms, "Oh…you're gonna get it!" And with one shift, he had me pinned underneath him. He lowered his lips to mine, and we hungrily kissed, our tongues dancing to their beats. Then, his lips were off mine, and his mouth roamed across my chest. He playfully touched his tongue to my right nipple, then started sucking feverishly on the peak.

"Oh my God…" I moaned, tossed my head back, and stared up at the ceiling as he took his exploration to new heights. I splayed my hands out on the bed and just laid there relishing the feel of his mouth on my nipples, as he searched out the right one and then the left. My fingers dug into the bedspread, and he slipped down my stomach, leaving a heated trail of kisses down my body until he reached my most tender region.

I bit back a groan, just waiting for him to arrive at his destination finally. When I felt his warm breath on my womanhood, I released a pleading whimper, then stilled myself. He ran his tongue along my hard nub, sending shivers down my spine. His tongue slid in and ever-so-slightly out. He pulled back, and the aching sensation he left had me wanting more then and forever. Matt planted soft kisses along my inner thighs, making me lift my hands to his hair and twirl my fingers around. I tried to push his lips back down to my nether lips, but he pulled back, leaving me wanting him more.

Pulling himself up, he hovered over me with a smirk. "How do you like that?"

"I love it, Matt," I said breathlessly.

He chuckled and lowered his mouth to mine.

"You'll be getting lots more of this. I'm just getting started with you, Tasha," he whispered just before he kissed me.

I spread my legs wider, and he fell into the space that naturally belonged to him, his erection knocking at the door of my womanhood, ready to come home. I twirled my fingers through his silky hair and held him close to me. He slowly moved in, pulled back, and then plunged inside of me, causing me to gasp between his lips.

Our rhythm intensified with each thrust, and my body was on immediate fire, as we crashed against one another, rocking our hips together in unison. He slowly expanded inside of me with me holding onto him tightly as he gave me so much pleasure.

"Yes!" I cried, squeezing my thighs together and locking him in our lovemaking mold.

Matt's rhythm forced me to crash into the bed with each thrust. His lips sought mine out often, settling in the soothing fashion of holding onto one another, clinging in desperation, and silencing our moans. He would slip out, then back in with thunderous desire, until our orgasms broke free, and we came together. When he pulled out of me, I sighed because I missed us being one.

Drifting to my shoulders, he kissed each one then snuggled against my neck, softly breathing against my skin. My heart raced so hard in my chest that I could barely control the pitter-patter. I ran my fingers down his back, covering each of his rigid muscles.

"I could get used to this," he said huskily.

"Me too."

Moving closer to him, I pressed my nakedness into his and he grabbed my arms to pull me into another heated kiss. When our lips parted from this kiss, we just stared at one another with admiration.

"This was one of the best days of my life, Tasha. Thank you."

"For what? It's me that's thankful for the invitation."

"Oh no, you could have turned me down. It's me that's the lucky one. I'm blessed that Dana referred you to work for me, and even more blessed that you accepted."

"I'm glad I lost my job at the right time, which just goes to show we never know when our blessings will come, or in what way they will come," I admitted.

"Baby, I'm blessed that you care so much about Cody, and it's just downright a gift from God that you choose to be with me, to give yourself to me. I love you, Tasha," he declared.

"I love you too, Matt." I kissed the top of his forehead before closing my eyes and snuggling up against him. I couldn't help it; the long trip from Colorado, the party, the sex had all drained me empty. I drifted off to sleep to the sound of Matt's breathing. It was a sound I could listen to forever.

***

I opened my eyes as the sun shone in the bedroom. I looked off to my side and found Matt soundly sleeping. I leaned in closer to him and took in a soft whiff of his woodsy scent. I touched my lips to his, sneaking feather kisses until he slid his hand up my back and lengthened the kiss.

"Hmmm…baby, I want to wake up like this every morning," he articulated groggily.

I moaned my approval, then pulled back and looked away. I wanted to mention something. Since Matt had been a bachelor for a long time, I didn't want him to think I was rushing things along with the question I wanted to ask.

"What's on your mind?" he asked, running his hand up and down my arm. I looked back at him, and he held the sincerest of smiles.

"I want you to come to Atlanta with me," I quickly stated.

He shrugged as if it was no big deal. "Sure, we can go to Atlanta. No problem. Is there a particular reason you want to go, or do you just like Atlanta?"

"It's my hometown," I advised him. "My family is there, and I would love for you to meet them." His eyes raised in surprise, and I worried that I was asking too much. "If you don't want to, and you think it's too early, then I completely understand."

"Shhh…" he whispered, brushing a finger along my shapely lips. "I would love to."

I leaned forward to kiss him, but as we kissed, it did bring me to ask another question. "So, I haven't heard about your parents. Do they live near, and are you close to them?"

His face clouded over with a stoic look. I could see the wall going up around him with each passing moment. "The only family you need to concern yourself with is Cody and my sister and brother-in-law that raised him until they died in a car wreck." With that, he got out of my bed as if the subject was finished.

"Baby, are you alright?" I asked.

"I'm fine."

"I'll drop it if it's a bad subject. I was just curious."

He turned around and faced me. "I had a good time last night." He started putting on his clothes. "But I think it's time that I leave."

"Matt, I'm sorry if I said something wrong. I didn't mean to—" I stopped when he held up his hand. All of this was confusing me. One minute we were trying to mold into one being, and the next, he seemed miles away from me emotionally.

"Tasha, there's no reason for you to be sorry. I'm just going to go out for an early breakfast and get some work done today."

"No, you're making excuses for not wanting to talk about your family. That's what you're doing. I understand if you don't feel comfortable enough to talk to me about them. I guess, after all this," I pointed at the crumpled-up sheets on my bed. "We just haven't reached that level yet. Maybe we shouldn't go to Atlanta to meet my family, either." I suspected I had gotten ahead of myself by inviting him to meet my family when he didn't feel comfortable talking to me about his.

"I'm sorry," he quickly apologized and sat back down on my bed, looking a bit calmer. "My dad left the picture when I was four, and my sister was two. When I turned eighteen, my mom died of breast cancer and Marisa and I were left alone. I raised her until she got married to Tony. So, this is it, Cody and myself, because no one else in my parents' families has made

120

an effort to reach out to me, and I'm inclined to return the favor."

I moved closer and palmed his face. "I'm sorry for asking about them, Matt. I had no idea," I said in a soft, comforting tone. His admission was the type of story that was hard to give any consolation for. "I didn't mean to push you, but hearing how you were there for your sister confirms what I already know: You are an amazing man."

The uncertainty in his eyes softened and his lips curved into a small smile. "It was a long time ago, but I don't like talking about it. I would be honored to meet your parents, though. Do you think they'll like me?"

I nodded. "Well, my mother would have loved you, but she passed away a few years ago from a heart attack, and I never really knew my father. My Aunt Clara and cousin Destiny are my closest family, and they will love you and Cody. I know they will, because they have been on me about finding someone for years, so at this point, they would be happy to see me show up with a puppy."

"Well, wait until they see this great catch you found," Matt teased with a smile.

I playfully hit his shoulder, then snaked my fingers around his neck to drag him closer to me. "You're right, I guess…" I taunted him.

Our lips connected in a slow kiss, which would be the start of a fire neither of us could put out until we were completely satiated.

Chapter Fifteen

Matt

Meeting with the Enemy

I took a drink from my glass of water and placed it down on the table. I had an important meeting where I was going to meet up with a high-profile rapper to discuss his case of celebrity vs. stalker. It was an open and shut case, as my client was suing for defamation of character and being stalked through the internet and most recently when they were on a family vacation. Given that all the evidence was right there on the web for all to see, I had no reason to believe he wouldn't win the case hands down.

Juice Luva was scheduled to meet me at my office, and he was already fifteen minutes late. I looked at my watch to confirm that he was indeed extremely late and was about to text his agent to see what the holdup was when I got a text message that he couldn't come into the office. Instead, he needed me to meet up with him at his studio.

I grunted and groaned my frustration, but it was the life I led. All my clients were high-end celebrities, and they were either bratty, catty, or bossy—sometimes all three at once. Therefore, I knew I had to make an effort to go to him if he couldn't make it to me. I grabbed my phone and briefcase, with all his paperwork, then took off out of my office. I had just gotten off the elevator when I spotted Melinda Lory coming through the front doors of the building.

Looking away from her, I hoped I could escape through a side door. I didn't want to talk to her, especially knowing everything she had done to Tasha. But she noticed me, and it was hard to get away from her clutches.

"Matt? Oh my God...what are you doing here?" Her voice was high-pitched and annoying.

I turned to glance at her. She knew very well what I was doing there; after all, she was aware I worked a few floors up.

"Hey, Melinda," I mumbled. "I think you know why I'm here, so the better question is, what are you doing here?"

She laughed haughtily and pat me on the arm. "Silly man, you know I'm the chief writer at *Colorful Times.* I have a meeting with one of the lawyers on your team."

"Yeah...I've heard about your job title. You haven't exactly kept it on the down-low."

"Well, if you have it...flaunt it." When she winked at me, I wanted to crawl in a hole.

"Gotta run! I have to meet up with a client, and I'm already late," I cut our little talk short and started to move past her, glad to make my escape.

She reached out and grabbed my arm to stop me. Her fingers dug into my elbow as she held onto it with a death grip. I turned back around to face her, then slowly pulled my arm away.

"I have to go, Melinda, but it was good seeing you." I lied to her, mainly so I didn't have to face her another minute.

The quicker I got out of there, the better I would be with keeping my promise to Tasha not to confront Melinda.

She moved closer to me and placed her hand to my chest, startling me by the intimate way she was now touching me. "We really should get together some time." She winked seductively.

I immediately brushed her off. "I don't think so, Melinda. I'm seeing Tasha, and I doubt she would like to know I was going out with another woman, especially if that woman was you."

Her jaw dropped slightly, then she laughed. "Tasha...Tasha Baker? I saw you two at the charity ball, but I didn't think that could ever be serious." She cozied up close to me to look me dead in the eye. "You really should rethink who you devote your time to."

Being a nice guy wasn't going to cut it, not when Melinda couldn't seem to understand that even if I wasn't seeing anyone, I would never play her games. I was tired of her snooping around, thinking I would entertain her when I wanted nothing to do with her. Fuck it. It was time to go nuclear on her no-good ass.

"You fired Tasha for no reason. Nina stole that story of hers, and you know it. So, now you come in here talking about being the head writer, which none of it impresses me because I know you got where you are by thievery."

Melinda touched the place over her heart and emitted a nervous laugh. "Oh...so she's telling lies now, is she?" she asked. I moved closer, cutting the distance between us. This movement made her smile. Then, her sneaky eyes dipped down to my lips and then back up to my eyes. "See, I knew you wanted me. It's alright to show it, Matt. We would make sweet love together if you stop letting her fill your head with foolishness."

Tasha couldn't stomach suing *Colorful Times* and Melinda because she didn't want a messy battle, but I wasn't Tasha. I took rogues to the cleaners for a living. By the time I got done with Melinda, she wouldn't be able to see straight enough to want me or any other man.

"Listen here, Melinda. You might have everyone else in this town fooled, but not me. I know you are jealous of the talent Tasha has, and now, she has the man you want, and it's burning you up inside."

"That's absurd. You're crazy, Matt."

"Oh, I bet you lay awake at night wondering why you're so inadequate, or why you're not getting enough attention. Well, if you keep barking up Tasha's tree, you might get the attention you're seeking. So, instead of coming on to me, which is not going to turn out the way you expect it to, you should watch your back. At some point, you might lose it all."

She smirked. "Are you threatening me, Matt Wilde?" she asked with her eyes filled with surprise. But even as she said those words, she looked like she enjoyed them a little too much.

I just shook my head at her desperation. "I'm not threatening you. I promise you, your day is coming." With that, I turned and left the building. On my way to my car, I dialed up Joseph Mallard's number.

"Hello, this is Stephanie, how may I direct your call?"

"Give me Mr. Mallard, please," I ordered.

"May I ask who's calling?"

"Tell him it's Matt Wilde."

"One moment, please."

Music played on the line as I unlocked my car door and slid into the driver's seat. He answered as I started my vehicle.

"This is Joseph Mallard."

"Hey, Joe…it's Matt Wilde."

"Hey, Matt. How's it going?"

I backed out of the parking spot with my phone call playing through the car's speakers. "I have something to discuss with you about two of your employees. Would you have some time later this afternoon to hear what I have to say?"

"This sounds serious."

"Yes, it is, and I'd rather discuss it in person."

"Okay, I could meet you at four-thirty. Will that work for you?"

"That'll work," I answered.

We finished setting up the appointment and said goodbye. Then, I continued my drive to the studio, thinking about how I needed to take care of this matter. I didn't want to worry Tasha with her old job, but she deserved to be happy, and I would do anything to make that happen, including dealing with a nagging crow deserving every bit of what was about to transpire.

***

"Mr. Mallard will see you now!" His secretary went back to her desk as I got up and headed to his office. This wasn't the first time I had been at his place of business. *Colorful Times* was only one of the many companies he owned. Over the years, we crossed paths a few times at networking mixers or when I represented clients for their advertisement contracts.

I knocked on the big man's door once I reached it.

"Come in!" he growled out, looking up from his computer. The minute I entered his office, he stood up from his desk to greet me. "Matt, it's good to see you," Joseph said, shaking my hand.

"Hello, Joe. Thanks for seeing me on such short notice."

I took my seat, and he joined me by sinking down into his chair. "It sounded urgent. What's on your mind?"

"It's come to my attention that one of your employees has violated copyright laws."

Joseph sat back in his chair with widened eyes. His hands, which were on his desk, joined together to form a diamond as he stared at me with disbelief. "That's a pretty big accusation there, Matt. Care to divulge more?"

I told him the whole story, everything Tasha shared with me, and how Melinda never showed remorse about it. I also told him about Nina and Melinda mocking Tasha at the charity ball. By the time I was done explaining the situation to him, I was left hoping I didn't leave any pertinent details out. I didn't want this to come across as a vendetta against women who had wronged my girlfriend, but what they did to Tasha was unethical, and quite frankly could land them in a world of trouble, if Tasha allowed me to go full blast with a case for her.

I sat there, waiting for his response. What came was a drawn-out sigh. I opened my mouth to question him but was cut off with his grateful reaction.

"Thank you for bringing this to my attention and for giving me the opportunity to right any wrong that may have been done. Secondly, Melinda Lory has had one of the most promising careers here at *Colorful Times*. I can't believe she would stoop so low as to doing something of this nature, so I will definitely have to look into this further, objectively."

He didn't want to get me started on what lengths Melinda would or wouldn't go to get what she perceived as hers. In the time I had known her, there wasn't anything she wasn't willing to try to get what she wanted. She was ruthless in her pursuit to the top, and that didn't always make for a good leader, especially when her employees couldn't trust her.

"So, Tasha told you about this?" he prodded.

I nodded, not wanting to explain why or how I learned about it, but I just wanted him to know that he could trust the information. "You know me, Joe, and you have for a long time. I wouldn't say any of this to you if I didn't know that it was legitimate. I don't fight dirty, and I don't rattle any unnecessary cages, but this one needs rattling. Tasha didn't get a fair shake."

Joseph nodded. "Your reputation is the reason that I'm listening to you. I trust that you wouldn't come to me with a half-ass argument. Tasha shouldn't have lost her job if someone snooped and got her stories from her. The fact is that I have noticed that the stuff coming from Nina's 'What's Up Now' column hasn't been as good as the story that got her the promotion. Her column has taken a free fall over the past month." He pondered all that, and I waited patiently to see what he would say next. "I'm going to look into it. If I find validity in what you say, I will be sure to take matters into my own hands, and Melinda or Nina won't get away with it."

"That's all I'm asking of you. Thank you." I stood to my feet, as Joseph got up. I reached out and shook his hand, hoping he would get to the bottom of it soon. "Will you call or text me when you decide what the next steps will be?"

"I will let you know." He walked me to his office door. "Thank you for coming in with this. You could have taken this in a different direction, so I appreciate the way you handled it, Matt."

After nodding in agreement, I headed down the hall and out of his office building. The plan was to take Melinda down a peg, or better, get Tasha back in her writing chair where she belonged with Melinda out on the street. As much as I would hate to see Tasha leave her babysitting post, and Cody would kill me for getting her old job back, I wanted her to do what made her happy.

Chapter Sixteen

Tasha

Welcome to Atlanta!

It wasn't easy finding the time where Cody was out of school and Matt could be off work, but eventually, we had a couple of days where we could head to Atlanta. Moving from Atlanta was one of the hardest decisions I made, but in the end, it was the right choice. Atlanta was a safe place for me, and I wanted to go somewhere where I could experience life without the comfort of my family or my hometown feel. Moving to Miami had been tough, but a great experience for me as a writer. Now, I was excited to be headed home to see the few family members I still had. On the trip there, I told Matt and Cody about my close-knit family.

"Ever since my mother passed away a few years ago, Aunt Clara has been my rock. She recently found her old love of her life, so we haven't talked much in the past few months, but you wait until you meet her. You'll know why she's so special to me."

Matt reached across my lap and touched my knee. "Baby, I'm going to love everyone in your family the same way I love you."

I gushed as I stared at him like a hopeless romantic. "I hope so, Matt. I just wish you could have met my mother." Her untimely death and her not being able to meet the man of my dreams dampened my mood a bit. "She would be tickled pink about me bringing a man home."

"I would have loved to meet her, even if she was only half as wonderful as you."

I smiled. "Yeah, it's hard losing a parent."

"I know. Have you ever thought about looking for your father?" he asked.

I shrugged. "He took off before I was born, so I don't know much about him, and since he hasn't looked for me all this time, I'd like to keep it that way."

"I can respect that," Matt said, dropping it.

"So, basically, while we're in Atlanta, you'll meet my Aunt Clara, my cousin Destiny, her husband Jacob, and my lovely niece and nephews."

"You have a tiny family like us, Tasha," Cody spoke up from the backseat.

I laughed and nodded. "That's right, I do, but the ones I have love me enough to make up for the numbers." I turned around and smiled at him. "Always remember, it doesn't matter the number of people you have in your corner, but the amount of love in your corner."

Cody nodded, casting a glance towards Matt. "I know what you mean." Cody lived in a small family with a lot of love.

When we arrived in Atlanta, we got our luggage and rental car, and within an hour, pulled into the driveway of Destiny and Jacob's home. I couldn't wait until the time came that I could get out of the car and run into Destiny's arms. We were like sisters growing up. Even though we hardly ever saw one another, every time we did, it was like no time had passed between us.

When Matt halted the car, I saw the door open, and Destiny stepped outside. I flung my passenger side door open and jumped out of the car, hurrying to greet her. I could hear Matt laughing in the background as she held one of her arms open in a welcoming fashion. The other held her bundle of joy, Jacob Jr.

After breaking away from the hug, I breathed in the Atlanta air, allowing the smell of home to fill my lungs. Smiling widely, I leaned down and kissed little Jacob's chubby leg, tugged at his chubby cheeks, then inhaled his little neck. "It's so good to see you, little cousin," I cooed. "He is just so precious and smells so good! I love babies."

"Thank you, Tasha. So good to see you, cuz," Destiny cheerily said before her eyes went to Matt. "Who do we have here?"

The rustling of feet on the pavement made me turn to Cody and Matt, who were lugging the suitcases to the porch. I beamed at Matt then turned back to Destiny. "This is my boyfriend, Matt, and his nephew, Cody."

Matt and then Cody greeted Destiny with hugs.

"Tasha has told me so much about both of you that I feel I already know you," Destiny divulged.

Matt chuckled. "I hope she didn't bore you with stories about me. I'm not exciting enough for conversation, I'm sure."

She snickered at Matt's attempt to be modest. "Not at all. They were all very intriguing." Not giving Matt a chance to respond, Destiny pointed to the bags he and Cody were carrying. "Bring those in, and I'll show you to the guestrooms."

Matt's eyes found mine, and I knew he wanted to know the 'intriguing stories' I'd told Destiny about him. We followed Destiny inside, and she showed us upstairs to the guest bedrooms. Cody walked inside his room and was awestruck.

"Whoa…where'd you get all this cool baseball stuff?" He touched a locked glass case holding a signed baseball, which was obviously a collectible and worth lots of money.

Everything in the room was most likely valuable since Destiny's husband, Jacob Turner, was CEO of the largest construction business in the United States. Just with the hurricanes in Texas and Florida, his company had been awarded a quarter-billion-dollar worth of contracts to repair and restore public buildings this year. The man could throw money away every morning and never go broke.

"It's my son's," Destiny told Cody. "He plays in this room when we don't have guests. Jacob is a baseball fan, so he keeps it stocked with whatever rare memorabilia he can find. When Montie Jr. gets home, he'll show you all around."

"Oh cool, Miss Tasha told me about Montie Jr. I can't wait to play with him."

Smiling lovingly, Destiny assured Cody. "Well, he's with his father right now, but he should be home by dinnertime."

"Yes, ma'am," Cody walked into the room and put his bag down.

"Your bedroom is over here," she said, pointing to Matt and myself. Cody stayed in his room while Matt and I went across the hall into another equally spacious room. This one was decorated with elegant earthy décor, mostly browns, tans, and ivory.

"What...no baseball memorabilia for us?" Matt joshed.

Laughing, I touched his arm and told Destiny, "This is perfect, cousin. Knowing you wouldn't have let us stay in a hotel, I thank you for putting us up for a couple of nights in style. I have wanted to come back to see you for a while now."

"Nope, I wouldn't hear of you staying at a hotel, not when I have more house than I can live in," she affirmed.

"I wish you were still in Miami so we could see each other more."

"Girl, I'm excited to have you here, but I felt it was best that we move back to Atlanta, all things considered." She gave me a knowing glance, and I nodded as she stepped back to the door. Her husband had a crazy stalker who had been admitted to a Miami mental facility, and the city just held terrible memories for Destiny. "Jacob will be home in an hour, and Mama won't be in until tomorrow. So, why don't you guys rest up and dinner will be ready in a little while?"

"Okay," Matt and I said in unison.

Before leaving out of the room, Destiny glanced back at me and said, "Glad to have you back."

"It's good to be home," was my reply.

Once alone, I caught Matt staring at me as if something was on his mind. "Why are you looking at me like that?"

He chuckled. "How am I looking at you?"

"As if you have something you want to say to me."

He grabbed my hand and pulled me to him, sweeping his warm breath across my lips. "She said it's good to have you home. Do you consider this home or back in Miami?"

The broader question simmering beneath his words piqued my interest. I felt at home with Matt, so wherever he was had become the new definition of home for me. After closing the door, I wrapped my arms around him and inched close enough to feel his body heat.

"Atlanta is my hometown officially. But this place stopped being my home when you and I started seeing each other. Now, home is wherever you are."

His mouth came crashing down on mine, and we kissed, his tongue igniting a duel, holding me as a captive to the war I undoubtedly lost this time around. I wanted to surrender to him until the sun set and rose again, but a knock on the door pulled us apart.

Cody's voice broke into the moment. "You guys in there?"

"To be continued," Matt whispered.

Nodding, I went to the door and opened it, and Cody started to talk about his room and how incredible the baseball collection was. I shot Matt a couple of sultry glances, and he just smiled and nodded at Cody's enthusiasm as he peeked at me from time to time to return the heat. I was glad to share moments like this with the two guys in my life.

***

Spending the evening with Destiny and Jacob was filled with good times. Aunt Clara's flight was delayed in Ireland, so she wouldn't make it back into the country until the next day. For the time being, it was the eight of us, including Cody, Montie Jr., Montana, and little Jacob Jr. cooing beside Destiny. I couldn't believe my cousin had a full family of five. She still seemed so vibrant, as if raising three kids wasn't driving her crazy. If I had three small kids ranging from newborn to seven, I would be losing it. Not her. She was the epitome of organization and grace.

Dinner was lovely, just talking and getting reacquainted with one another. We then went into the living room and continued to catch up, which bored Cody and Montie Jr. to no end. About an hour in, they said they wanted to go to bed. Montana and Jacob Jr. had already crashed for the night and were sleeping soundly in their rooms.

"Do you want me to come up and tuck you in?" Matt asked Cody.

Cody shot a disbelieving look at Matt. "Uncle Matt...seriously?"

That started laughter amongst the four adults. "Sorry. Have a good night!" corrected Matt.

"Well, you know you're getting tucked in Montie Jr., so don't even try it," Jacob said to my little cousin.

"Yeah, you're not even in the double digits, yet, so tucking in is a must," I chimed, rubbing Montie Jr.'s wavy, black hair.

"I know, Cousin Tasha. I like to be tucked in," Montie Jr. said and hugged me. Then, he ran up to Cody. "Come on, let me show you my trainset."

"Oh, cool!" Cody headed out of the living room, bounding up the stairs behind Montie Jr.

"Good night," Destiny called after them, and that caused them to turn around.

"Good night," said Cody.

"Good night, Mama," Montie Jr. mimicked then his eyes scanned the room. "Good night, everyone." He then ran on upstairs, eager to show Cody his trainset.

Watching the boys disappear at the top of the steps, I heard Destiny say, "Matt, you have a great nephew. You raised him well."

Matt beamed with well-deserved pride. "Thank you, but my sister had a big hand in that. I just helped raise the smart young man she already molded."

Smiling, Destiny looked at Jacob with joy in her eyes.

Jacob beamed as he reached over and took Destiny's hand into his before kissing the back of it. "That's how I feel about my stepchildren, Junior and Montana. They come from a beautiful mold. I'm just blessed to be in their lives."

Destiny leaned in, and Jacob met her halfway for a heated kiss. Momentarily, they were so wrapped up into each other, it seemed as if they forgot we were there. When Jacob released her hand to palm the sides of her face, deepening the kiss, Destiny's hands went to his shirt to grip it as if she needed something to hold onto so as not to lose her balance in her seat.

"Whew," she breathily said once Jacob let her lips go and ran the pad of his finger across them.

"I mean every word, baby," he assured her in an impassioned tone.

The heated looks they imparted on one another let me know their passion was still as strong as ever. My cousin loved her husband to no end, and everyone who knew them personally knew it.

"You have a nice and big family, and I can tell it was made out of love," Matt said to Jacob, though his eyes were only on me. "I can't wait to have a little one of my own running around the house. I might just have a small football team someday," Matt intimated, still looking at me, trying to gauge my response.

Thoughts of all the times we had sex without a condom roamed through my mind. *Let's hope my birth control is one hundred percent right now,* I thought, as he continued stating his wishes about having a large family. We hadn't talked about having children, much less the incubation of an entire football team.

"I feel sorry for whoever you hire to work in your baby-making factory," I quipped.

"Oh, I already have the perfect person working in that position," Matt shot back.

"Girl, you're going to be busy," Destiny chimed in, laughing and taking Matt's side in his obvious joke.

"That's too bad, but I wish you good luck with that, Matt." I laughed nervously because his eyes held a hint of seriousness.

We talked a little while longer until I began to yawn. "I hate to be an old head, but I should get in bed since I can't quit yawning," I told Destiny.

"It has been a very long day, and we both need our rest," Matt agreed. "Thanks again for letting us stay here. We could have rented a room, but your hospitality would have never been matched."

"You're welcome here anytime, and you both have a good night!" Destiny happily said. She and Jacob waved as Matt and I headed up the steps and to our bedroom.

When the door closed behind us, I grabbed ahold of Matt's shirt and pulled him to me. "How about you hire me for this baby-making job tonight?"

He laughed, pressing me against the bedroom door and wrapping his arms firmly around me. Kissing me roughly, his body pressed into mine as I lifted my leg around his.

"You got the job, baby," he whispered huskily against my ear. "Can you handle it?"

I pushed him back, grabbed onto my shirt, and pulled it over my head, tossing it to the floor. He moved closer to me and unclasped my bra, threw it, and grabbed my waist. Lowering his mouth to my breasts, he massaged my nipples with his thumbs while he trailed kisses up and down my cleavage. I pulled my pants down and kicked out of them, as he devoured my breasts.

Matt moved back to my mouth, kissing me senseless as he maneuvered us to the bed. Breaking free from the kiss, he looked at me with this macho grin as I crawled on top and straddled him. My fingers traveled to the waist of my panties, sliding them down.

"Damn, baby. You're so hot tonight," he moaned.

Grabbing onto the bottom of his shirt, I pulled it up to his chest and over his head. I planted my lips on his now bare chest.

Lurching, he gripped the back of my neck while I scattered kisses across his chest. Then, I started to undo the buttons of his pants. When I got his pants undone, I moved my lips down his stomach, slid his boxers down some, and placed a kiss on his dick.

"God, baby, they're going to hear you screaming," he whispered.

I pulled his boxers down and tore them off him. He laughed and twitched beneath me. Then, I went back to giving his erection the attention it deserved. "Not before they hear you," I said with a devilish wink.

Running my tongue down his elongated shaft as he grabbed my hair, I moved my tongue up and down his length. Matt's moans bounced off the walls when I flicked my tongue over the tip to capture his precum. He let out a loud breath as he ran his fingers in my hair, and I sucked quicker with him slowly thrusting into my mouth.

"UGH!" he groaned as he was near eruption. "Tasha, baby!"

Wanting to release with him, I greedily straddled him, positioning my throbbing pussy above his hardness.

Grabbing my hair roughly, he tugged at the silky strands, hauling me to him for a kiss, and our tongues wildly danced.

I rocked my hips as Matt pounded in and out of me until his orgasm jetted out of him, coating my core with life. Electric waves ran through me. Joining him in bliss, he wrapped me in his warm embrace and held me as I collapsed atop of him, spent.

Matt's words came out in a murmur. "How have I survived without you?"

Resting my head to his shoulder, I replied, "I don't know..." And I really didn't know how I made it a day without him. Drifting off to sleep, I was feeling good when Matt nudged me.

"Tasha, I have something to tell you."

"What is it, baby?"

He spoke slowly and thoughtfully when he informed me, "I spoke with Joseph Mallard."

I sprang up straight in the bed, frowning as I recognized the name. "The owner of *Colorful Times*?" I had to be sure.

Nodding, he continued to explain, "Yes, I told him what happened with your column."

Literally, I could feel my face falling. I couldn't comprehend why Matt had taken it upon himself to talk to my ex-boss. "You went behind my back and talked to him. I asked you not to do that."

Not addressing my statement, Matt informed me, "I got a text from him a little while ago, and I was waiting to tell you at the perfect time that he wants to hire you back."

It took me a while to process what he was saying to me.

"Well, you didn't get your old job back. Actually, you will be promoted to head writer. That's if you still want to work there."

My jaw hung open in complete shock. What was Matt saying to me?

"This has to be some kind of sick joke, right?"

He shook his head. "Absolutely not. I wouldn't joke about something this serious. Joseph Mallard will call you next week to discuss the details with you. I should have told you, but I was waiting—" His words entered my mouth when I kissed him. "...for the right time."

"This is the perfect time, Matt. Of course, I want to know all of the details, but I will happily talk to Mr. Mallard.

But what happens with the two wicked witches—Melinda and Nina?"

"Well, let's just say you won't have to worry about them anymore because they're—"

A knock at the door interrupted Matt's answer. We scrambled to cover ourselves before answering it.

"Yes?" I called out.

"It's me, Destiny. Jacob and I are about to go to bed. Checking to make sure you guys have everything you need tonight," she asked in a hushed voice so as not to wake up the sleeping children.

Matt and I looked at each other mischievously.

"We have everything we need. Thank you!" I told her.

"Okay, see you guys in the morning. Goodnight."

"Goodnight, Destiny."

As soon as we heard Destiny's footsteps padding down the hallway, Matt finished his statement. "They're fired, baby. You don't have to worry about them anymore."

To say I was happy would be an understatement. "I don't know how you pulled off getting rid of the evil twins and getting my job back, but we can talk more about it tomorrow. Right now, I just want to thank you for standing up for me because I know you did something to right their wrongs, and I will never take you for granted, Matt, never," I whispered as I crawled on top of him, feeling revived and ready to make love to him as if I wasn't exhausted already.

Chapter Seventeen

Matt

Reliving History

"Goodbye, sweetheart. You've got yourself a kindred spirit in Matt. Take care of him, and he will take care of you," Tasha's aunt said. That made me smile. She was supposedly whispering, but I could hear her while I sat in the car waiting for Tasha, with the music playing softly. Things went better than I could have hoped for, as our Atlanta trip came to an end.

"Thanks, Aunt Clara. I wish we could have spent more time together." Tasha hugged her aunt's neck.

"Yeah, but those damn Irish tried to keep us over there as immigrants." She laughed. "I thought I was going to have to nut up if they didn't let us get on a plane, but John handled everything and got us here in time to see you before you left. You know he's the saner of the two of us."

John, who was Jacob's father, put an arm around Tasha's aunt and pulled her close to his side. "I wasn't going to let her miss you," he said. John reached his free hand into my window and shook my hand. "Nice to meet you, Matthew. The next time I'm in Miami, I'll look you up so that we can play a few holes."

"That would be great. I'd like that," I said, smiling at the old man who was the spitting image of Jacob, only more distinguished.

143

After everyone had hugged and said their goodbyes, including Montie Jr. and Cody, we headed back to the airport. I enjoyed seeing her so happy, and even as we left the city, she still held a smile on her face. It was evident Tasha was okay with leaving Atlanta and heading back with us. I looked over at her and watched as she looked out the window. We hit the highway to get back to our home. Soon, we endured a quick flight and landed in Miami. I had a great time in Atlanta, but nothing compared to the sight of the "Welcome to Miami" sign hanging over my city.

"It was great meeting your cousin, her husband, and your aunt. I had a great time."

"So did I," Cody said, piping up from the backseat.

Tasha turned and looked at us. "I'm glad you had a good time. I'm glad we all went." She reached over and grabbed my hand, and we held hands all the way back to her place. I would have offered again for her to stay with us, but she told me several times she needed to go to her apartment to tidy it up. When I pulled into the parking lot of her apartment complex, I grabbed the nearest spot to her building.

"I'll walk you upstairs."

"Okay." She turned back to look at Cody. "See you later, Cody!"

"Are you coming over for dinner?" Cody asked, an excited look playing in his expressions.

She looked at me, and I tried to portray eagerly that that was exactly what I wanted while responding in her place. "I'll certainly try to persuade her to, buddy." Then, I laughed and got out of my car. I went around and got Tasha's suitcase, and we walked to her apartment building.

"So…dinner, huh?" she asked, laughing slightly.

"You know I would love for you to come over when you get done here. But I also know you need time alone sometimes. I don't want to crowd you." 'Unless you want to be crowded' was implied.

We went upstairs to her apartment. When we reached her door, she turned to me. There was a gleam in her eye. "I do have to eat, you know." She laughed, and I dropped the suitcase and snickered, brushing my hand against her cheek.

"That you do. But another thing I was thinking about," I started. "You know, it seems kind of silly for you to still be living here. You should move in with Cody and me."

The minute the words left my mouth, I was surprised I said them aloud. I was unequivocally in love with Tasha, but moving in was the next level. Her eyes widened, and her mouth hung open. I playfully touched the area of her chin close to her mouth.

She giggled coyly. "I'm sorry. I wasn't expecting that."

"Honestly, I wasn't expecting it either."

She cocked her head to the side, questioning my motive with her intense brown eyes.

Eager to explain, I said, "I mean that moving in with one another is a big step. A lot is happening in both our lives, and we have to make sure that it'll blend. I do not doubt that it will, because I do love you."

"And I love you, and when the time is right, then I would be all for it, but you're right. It's a bit premature. We have Cody to think about and while I know Cody likes me—"

"He loves you," I rectified.

Her smooth, brown hand inched up and covered her heart. Swallowing the lump in her throat, she said, "And, I love him too, Matt. I do. But he's young, and to protect his feelings, we should take things slow. Agreed?"

She was right to consider Cody's feelings. That was what I'd done since he came to live with me a few years ago. Before I met Tasha, I wore my emotions on my sleeve and dusted my shoulders off regularly, but now, I was ready to invite Tasha in and share my and Cody's world with her. However, I wouldn't and couldn't do that a minute before she was ready.

Leaning in to kiss her, I agreed with her. "Agreed, Tasha, but we'll rehash the issue soon." *I need you with me...*

She breathed out an exasperated sigh, letting me know she didn't want our kiss to end. "I'll be over at six for dinner?" she said as more of a question.

"I'll be counting down the minutes."

I waited for her to open her door, then watched her go inside.

Once in the car, Cody asked, "Is she coming?"

"She'll be there at six."

He did a celebratory dance in the backseat as I started the car and backed out of my parking spot. All the while, I was anticipating and mentally celebrating Tasha's return to us, as well.

When I pulled into the driveway, I had a lot of things to do before Tasha arrived.

"Take your suitcase, go in, and unpack, Cody."

"Sure thing, Uncle Matt." He grabbed his suitcase and hurriedly ran off toward his bedroom.

146

After pulling out my bag, I went to the mailbox and grabbed the mail for the past couple of days. Fumbling with my suitcase and the mail, I went up to the front door. Cody left the door wide open, so I walked right in.

Once in the house, I dropped my suitcase and leafed through the mail. Besides bills, bills, and more bills, there was a package addressed to me with no return address. The block lettering wasn't recognizable, but I opened the box and found a DVD. Inside the DVD casing was a letter written in block print, reading:

Watch this, and you will see your precious girlfriend isn't as innocent as you think. She will do anything for a dollar. Consider yourself warned.

I read through the note twice and frowned at the conclusion. It didn't make any sense to me. I was worried about watching the DVD but then reminded myself I had nothing to worry about. Whatever was on the DVD meant nothing. Tasha and I had a stable relationship, and anything in this box wouldn't change that, at least that was what I hoped.

Just watch it. You don't know what's on there, so you can't consciously say that. My mind kept trying to warn me that something horrible could be on there. I contemplated whether I wanted even to watch it, but I knew that I had to, because I wouldn't be able to think about anything else if I didn't. I looked up the stairs to make sure Cody was still up there. When I was sure he was in his room, I went to the den. Nerves slowly took root.

I stood at the DVD player, a disc in hand, and again considered not playing it but dropped it in the player and turned it on anyway. I stepped back from the TV and pushed play. I had to wait for it to warm up, but once it did, the first sounds I heard were moaning. Once a haze left the screen, I was met with an instant porno.

My mouth hung open. I stared at the screen in front of me. Two people were having sex for the camera. I wanted to ask what this had to do with Tasha. Then, it became apparent. The woman moaning out in pleasure was the love of my life, my future wife. I looked away from the screen, my heart racing as I wondered why she would want to stoop so low as to make a sex tape. Then, I wondered who was on the receiving end.

The note read that she would do anything to get what she wants. I muted the sound, so Cody couldn't hear, then turned back to the screen to watch the scene play out. I don't know why I kept watching, other than it was like a bad accident on the highway; you're horrified, but you must see what happens. I worked overtime, mentally, trying to figure out why she would hit that level, and who and why would they send me some mess like this.

"Uncle Matt?"

I panicked and quickly turned the TV off, then shot a look at Cody. "What do you want?" I snapped.

His eyes got big, and I was sorry that I snapped at him like that. "I, uh…" he stammered. He glanced at the screen, but luckily, I had gotten it turned off in time.

"I'm sorry," I apologized. "What's going on, bud?" I asked in a much calmer tone.

"What's for supper?" His voice was shaky. I had never yelled at him like that before, and he had to be thinking that something was seriously wrong. Something was wrong; I just learned that Tasha made a sex tape and that it was circulating.

148

"I thought I would throw on steaks." Still managing to maintain the calm façade, I had a fire brewing deep inside of me that I had to fight with all that was in me to water it down.

Cody nodded, still looking at me as if he were in shock over my initial blow up. "Okay…And Tasha is still coming, right?"

Yeah, back to Tasha. I remembered being so happy that she was coming to have dinner with us. After the trip to Atlanta and everything we shared, I wanted to believe we were meant to be together, grow old together, with our very own family. Now, I was left wondering if I even knew what kind of woman she was.

"Yeah, man, she'll be here." Forcing a smile was meant to hide the serious doubts swirling through my mind about the woman that was quickly becoming his favorite person. Cody loved Tasha. I knew that, and it would break his heart if something happened between us, but I also had to think about how this would affect him. It wasn't a cut and dry scenario. I needed some quiet time to think. "Go get washed up. Dinner will be ready in just a bit."

Cody ran off, seemingly happy again. I wanted to keep it that way. Once he was gone, I turned back to the TV and turned it back on. I was again greeted by the horrible view of the couple having sex, wondering if I could at least count on this being an ex-boyfriend of hers. But then as they finished the climax and she collapsed on top of him, the scene changed. This time, there were only pictures. Half-naked pictures were displayed on the screen. Tasha smiled as she posed for these pictures, and she looked proud to do it.

My heart fell. Not only did she have a sex video made, but she was now posing for near-nude shots. Did she do it for the money? When did she do it? If she needed money, I could halfway understand that, but why pimp herself out?

I couldn't even watch the whole thing as more and more of her body was exposed. No decent woman should have these views of her sent through the mail. I turned the TV off and went over, nearly yanking the DVD from the player. I put it away, leaving the letter on the outside. I didn't know who the message was from, but it was apparently from someone that hated Tasha so much, and the thought hit me. Only Melinda had that much vengeance towards her, as to direct it at me, at least so I figured.

I fell back on the couch and just sat there, dumbfounded by the revelation. I don't know how long I sat there, but when I heard her voice, I didn't even realize how much time had passed.

"Matt, hey there!" She giggled like a lovesick young lady when she spoke to me, but I wasn't feeling the love right then. I kept staring at the blank TV screen. "I knocked, but you didn't come, so I let myself in. I hope that's alright." Obviously picking up on my mood, her tone was also changing.

I slowly turned to her, had been practicing the words I would say to her in my head since I watched the DVD. I planned to let her know how I felt, then tell her we had to slow things down drastically until I knew her better. But as I looked at her, I couldn't even get those words out of my mouth.

She frowned. "Matt, is everything alright, babe?"

"Um…well, not exactly." I stood from the couch and walked over to her. I looked past her and peered up the steps,

150

making sure Cody couldn't hear us, then grabbed her hand and pulled her further into the living room. "I need to talk to you."

"You're scaring me," she softly said, then a nervous chuckle accompanied her words. "What's going on?"

I swallowed the lump in my throat. "That's what I'm wondering," I said, holding up the DVD. "This came in my mail today. Care to explain what I saw?" I kept my voice low so it wouldn't trigger Cody to come downstairs, investigating.

Her eyes narrowed in on the disc in my hand. "Well, first of all, what's the DVD of?" She looked at me with confusion etched on her face.

The scene came back to my mind, and I shook my head, wanting to erase it forever. "It's of you and some guy," I hissed. "Then half-naked photos of you." I thrust the disc towards her. My anger boiled over. I was unable to think straight.

Her eyes widened as she grabbed the disc from me. "I don't understand. What are you talking about?"

I took a deep breath and wanted nothing more but to stay calm and relaxed about it, because this was the woman I loved, and I wanted to trust her and believe anything she had to tell me. However, my thoughts were clouded, and I really couldn't picture her telling me anything that would make this okay.

"I got this note." I opened it up and held it open to her.

She read through it, and her eyes went dim. The brightness I saw when I looked at her before was gone.

"Matt…I can explain," she said dejectedly.

Those might've been the worse words she could've said to me right then. Explaining meant this wasn't a joke, the film wasn't a fake.

I shoved the paper into her hand and shook my head. "I doubt you can, but give it your best shot." I moved past her, prepared to open the door, kick her out, and never look back, even if my heart was breaking with the thought of it.

"Matt, listen. It's not as bad as it looks."

Slowly, I closed the distance between us. "Are you sure about that? It looks pretty damn bad, and let's talk about humiliating. If it got out that my girlfriend made a sex tape and posed nude…"

"I wasn't nude," she quietly stated.

"Oh…I stand corrected. HALF nude! You know, I can't be a hard nose attorney, when I can't even handle a relationship. If that DVD got out, then I would be the laughingstock of the city. No one would want to have me represent them. My career could be finished. I guess you'd finally be the topic of all the popular blogs then," I growled out the latter, wishing I could suck the words back into my lips and swallow them down to the deepest and darkest places of me I never wanted the world to see.

"They won't find out," she said, and her chest began to heave up and down. I could see the pain in her pleading eyes, which searched for the compassionate, understanding guy she'd grown to love, but all I could see was the downside of this video—along with seeing red.

"Oh yeah, how do you plan to stop them when it ended up in my mailbox?" I pressed.

"Matt, that video was shot a long time ago, so even if someone does leak it to the blogs, it's from when I was younger," she said. "I was just getting into the writing industry and—"

I shook my head and put up my hand to stop her. "I don't want to hear about it. I mean it, Tasha. There's nothing you could say that would make this better." Tears had started to form in the corner of her eyes. I wasn't a monster; I hated seeing her like that, but the situation gave me no choice. I looked away from her. "I think you should go."

Out the corner of my eye, I saw her nod. "Yeah, I really should. I never thought you would be such a judgmental asshole!"

"Oh yeah? Well, I guess that makes two of us who've been duped because I never thought I would receive a porno in the mail with you starring in it." I turned away from her and led her out of the living room, feeling like I was walking in quicksand that was pulling me down fast. I internally damned Melinda Lory for being the evil witch of the south who I was sure was behind dropping this bomb in the middle of the damn near perfectness that had become Tasha and me.

We had just reached the door when I heard Cody's footsteps. I turned around and looked up to find him bouncing down the stairs, a huge smile spread across his face.

"Hey, Tasha, did you hear that we're going to have…" his face fell as he reached us. His eyes homed in on her and probably noted the tears flowing down her cheeks. "Is something wrong?" He looked at the door and the fact that we were heading to it. "Are you leaving?"

Tasha smiled and looked down at him, still with tears in the backs of her eyes. "Hey, little man." She knelt in front of him, and I was forced to watch the beginning of her breaking up with him. "You know how I love you, right?"

He nodded, and that was all I could take. I couldn't let her walk out the door, not right then and break Cody's heart like she had broken mine.

"She wasn't leaving, Cody."

Tasha looked at me wide-eyed as if she were silently asking what I was doing.

"She was about to grab something from the car, right, Tasha?

She tilted her head to the side, trying to read me, then slowly nodded. "Yes, like your Uncle Matt said, I left my phone out in the car."

"While you grab your phone, Cody and I will get those steaks started, okay?" I pleaded with my eyes for her to go along with my story.

Tasha stared back at me, and she seemed confused, but so was I. Her eyes went from me to Cody.

"I'll be right back." She darted to the door, wiping away tears.

I wanted to go after her, pull her into my arms, and tell her everything would be okay, but I wasn't so sure it would be. I wasn't sure of anything after watching that video.

I just knew I couldn't let her leave when Cody was looking forward to it. Yeah, that was what I told myself. That I was pleading with my eyes for her to stay because of Cody, and that I would figure out what we needed to do later. For now, I had food to prepare, and my separation from Tasha was prolonged until after dinner.

Chapter Eighteen

Tasha

Finality

Dinner with my two favorite guys would be short-lived. Matt wasn't going to let this home video ordeal go away without consequences, and my mind kept reeling, trying to figure out how it got in his possession. Who would stoop so low as to send it to him in the mail? I thought all copies of that disastrous event were destroyed, but Melinda associated with my spiteful ex, Harper Finley—a man I spent every day since I laid eyes on that home movie the first time years ago trying to forget. She had to be the one to stoop this low.

When my relationship with Harper blew up over the tape, Melinda caught wind of it and apparently had also gotten her hands on a copy of the video he took of us together. She was probably tickled pink, knowing the carnage she was causing to my heart right now. She had it out for me, and seeing me happy with Matt made her want to do something to wreck us, and sending a wrecking ball our way fast and furiously was what she did. After Matt got her fired from her job for terminating me—wrongfully, I might add—she must've spent her days digging up all the dirt she could find. It had become apparent she would do anything to seek revenge.

"Tasha? Tasha?" Cody was calling out my name.

I shook out of my haze of thoughts and focused on him. "I'm sorry, bud. What'd you say?" I could feel Matt's stare on me as I answered Cody. His thoughtful gazes were making me feel as awkward as I did the day he found out the fire department had come to his house.

"I was talking about the great time I had in Atlanta. Are we going to go back?"

I didn't want to spoil anything for the little guy, who had become so comfortable with my family, so I glanced at Matt to give him a nudge to help me out with my reply. Matt nodded, letting me know he didn't want Cody to suspect anything was off between us. I knew he didn't want Cody to deal with the pain of loss again, and that showed his big heart, but it also gave Cody a false sense of security if, eventually, he was going to break things off with me over Melinda butting into our lives.

"Little man, I would love for us to go back to Atlanta." That was the truth. "My family wants to see you again, too, especially Montie Jr."

The beam in his eyes caused sadness in mine. Everything I loved was washing away in a matter of minutes. I knew this would be our last dinner together. As if on cue, Matt stood from the table and started to clear away the empty dishes, bringing the end nearer.

"I'll help," I mumbled, trying to be uplifting and positive…and a bit fake because I felt neither.

"Don't bother. Just enjoy your time with Cody, Tasha," Matt issued dryly as he moved away from the table quickly.

Ouch! His encouragement to enjoy the time I had left with Cody felt like a slap.

"I was wondering when I could invite my friends over again. They've been pressuring me about it." Excitement filled his boyish voice, bringing another pained smile to my face.

I would have promised him another playdate, but I couldn't since I knew the fate of my relationship with Matt therefore Cody.

"Well, that does sound like fun," was my reply. "We'll have to see if we can make that happen."

Cody pumped his fists in the air. "Yeah! This time, we can go to the arcade!"

Matt came back to the table and instructed Cody to, "Go get washed up and ready for bed, my man."

"Uncle Matt..." Cody groaned. "A few more minutes, please...please..."

One raise of Matt's eyebrow halted Cody's whining.

I pulled the adorable young boy, who I had come to love, into my arms for a warm hug. Tears threatened to seep out their sockets as I embraced his tiny frame.

"Goodnight, Cody. Sleep tight...don't let the bed bugs bite."

He giggled, his laughter making me feel a little better. "Goodnight, Tasha."

I squeezed him tighter than ever before. "I love you, Cody. I want you to know that."

"I love you too!" When he pulled back, he looked at me, giving me a second glance before leaving the dining room. When he disappeared, it felt as if the comfort I had come to treasure was being ripped from me, the same way I wanted to remove Melinda Lory from her limbs.

"I guess I will leave now," I mumbled without looking in Matt's direction. I could feel his presence following me as I walked to the door and then outside. It was the longest walk to my car, but when I got there, I turned to face him. "I'm not this horrible person you think I am. Will you allow me to explain what you saw on that tape?"

He shook his head. "I don't think you're horrible, Tasha. You might have made a bad decision, but you're not horrible."

"I didn't make a bad decision...that's just it. You're getting one side of the story," I argued. It was crappy that he wasn't giving me that chance to explain.

When he shook his head again, my world crumbled. "I don't need you to explain what I saw on that tape. For one, you shouldn't have to explain. If I can't trust who I thought you were, then I can't trust you."

Those words were like scalding hot water being thrown at me. I never intentionally gave Matt a reason not to trust me, and if he would hear me out, I was sure I could regain that trust. Except, he didn't want to hear me out.

"Tasha, I've always been responsible and worked hard to stay on top. That hard work has landed me a growing business that's prominent in this city. People look up to me to always do the right thing. Cody is of an age that he looks up to me for the same. He needs positive role models in his life, and what I saw today doesn't promote that. Sorry."

Falling against the car, blow after blow barreled from the mouth of a man I thought would never strike me so painfully.

"I'm sorry you feel that way, and I'm sorry that this happened. If I could take back anything, I would take back knowing the person who filmed me. But, you should know, I would never do anything to harm Cody. If you feel my being around him would jeopardize him, then I'll walk away without hesitation." A sob released from my throat, and I willed myself not to cry aloud, but it had already begun. "I'm sorry, Matt."

Opening the door to my car, I hopped in before he had a chance to stop me. As I backed out, I noticed he wasn't going to stop me anyway. I didn't know if I could ever get over the pain of seeing the disappointment in his eyes. So many tears released along with a ripple of uncontrollable trembles through me. My past had come back to bite me once again.

***

The minute I got home, I shredded the DVD. I hoped that it was the last one of its kind, but with the snakes I had to deal with, I doubted it seriously. I didn't need to watch it to know what was on it, but the fact remained that Matt never allowed me to explain myself, and that caused me to weep freely within the confines of my apartment.

The next three days were spent wrapped up in my covers, feeling sorry for myself. Every time I closed my eyes, I saw Matt or Cody and fell deeper into my sadness. Dana called a couple of times, but I ignored her until I got a text from her.

Dana: I know what happened with you and Matt. Please call me!

I was embarrassed. This should have been behind me, and now Harper's video was back at the surface again. I hated rehashing bad memories and decided to reply to Dana.

Me: I don't want to talk about it. Give me some space for now please.

Fifteen minutes after sending the message, I groaned because my phone was ringing. For sure, it was Dana wanting to talk.

"I told you I need some time and space before I can talk about it, Dana."

Hesitation came through on the other end of the line.

"Um…is this Tasha Baker?"

"Yeah!" I quickly stated, sitting up in my bed. I kicked myself for not looking at the caller ID. "This is Tasha."

"Hello Tasha, this is Joseph Mallard."

I recalled Matt telling me I should be hearing from him soon. "Oh, hello, Mr. Mallard. Sorry about that. I thought you were someone else, but hey…how may I help you?"

"I'm assuming that Matthew mentioned to you I would be calling."

"Um…yes…he did."

"Well, then you know I have reviewed the situation surrounding your termination, and I'm not happy with what happened to you. That's why I'm calling to offer you your job back officially, but this time as head writer."

"Oh, wow! I mean, I'm glad you called me," I said, fumbling for the right words to say. The ones I wanted to stay wouldn't come out. Like, 'I was treated horribly and, had I not been treated horribly by your employees, I wouldn't have started working for Matt and fell irreversibly in love with him, only to be mistreated further by your employees who sent him a sex tape and caused me to lose him and fall into the sunken place of heartbreak, forever.' But, I didn't say any of those things. Instead, I thanked him. "I appreciate you looking into my termination, Mr. Mallard. I am so grateful and would love to accept the offer." I sat up straighter and looked down at my pajamas, which I had been wearing every day since I left Matt's.

His booming chuckle filled the line. "Great! Can you start tomorrow? I mean, I'm a little short-staffed with the firings that have taken place."

"Tomorrow will be great!"

"Good, I will see you then."

I thanked him and hung up. Getting my old job back was the sign I needed to force me to stop wallowing in my pain over my failed relationship and to get on with my life. But, at the very least, I owed Matt another thank you for putting me in this position.

Pulling up his number, I began to shoot him a message.

Just got a call from Joseph Mallard. I start the job tomorrow. I—

The blood drained from my face. It was so easy to want to share this news with him, but I couldn't finish typing it. Would he really want to hear from me?

Definitely not.

I quickly erased the text with a familiar flow of butterflies in my stomach. Staring at the phone, it started ringing, and Dana's name flashed on the screen.

"Hello?"

"Well, it's about time you answered the phone," she fussed. "What's this I hear about you not working for Mr. Wilde anymore? What happened?"

Relieved she didn't know *why* I was fired—well, I wasn't officially fired since Matt never said the words to me—I knew Matt hadn't discussed the details with her.

"It's a long story," I said on a heavy sigh. "But I do, at least, have some good news to report. Mr. Mallard from *Colorful Times* just called me and gave me my old job back, even promoted me to head writer."

Dana's squeal through the phone vibrated through me, causing goosebumps on my skin. "This requires a celebration, Miss Head Writer. Let's meet for lunch and discuss what happened with Mr. Wilde and your new position."

Glad I still had someone to share my bright spot with, I willingly agreed. Again, I couldn't shake the feeling of doom from not talking to Matt.

Hanging up, I got out of bed, deciding not to dwell on the negative aspects of my life. Being a head writer had been my dream job, and now I had it. But things had changed, and the position I lost as Matt's other half was far more critical than any writing job could ever be.

Chapter Nineteen

Matt

Regrets

Weeks went by, and every day, my conscience beckoned for me to call her. I didn't like the way things ended. I wished we had a decent goodbye, but it was the only choice I had. If I could have those moments back, I would tell her I wasn't disappointed in her, and I would listen to what she had to say. She left thinking I had ill feelings towards her, and I don't know what I was thinking to let her drive away like that.

Barely noticing the time, I was thankful Mary stuck her head in the door to remind me Cody would be getting out of school soon. Giving her an appreciative smile, I said, "Thanks, Mary. What would I do without you?"

What I had been doing without Tasha was dying inside.

Mary's shoulders lifted in nonchalance. "Hope you never have to find out, Mr. Wilde."

"Me either." I grabbed my car keys and hurried out of the office.

Since Tasha wasn't around anymore, I took on the responsibility of picking up Cody from school. Pulling in front of the school as students started filtering out of the building, I kept my eyes peeled for Cody, inching my car up as other cars drove away. Eventually, I saw him coming out of the building.

Narrowing my eyes to see who was walking with him, the closer they got, the more I realized the kid looked familiar. I watched them interact when they stopped about ten feet from the car and continued talking. Saying goodbye, they did a boyish handshake, ending in a high five. Cody headed over to the car, opened the back door, and tossed his bookbag inside, followed by him hopping in and shutting the door.

Looking at him through my rearview mirror, I asked, "How was school today?"

He shrugged. "Fine. School is school."

"So, wasn't that Bobby, the kid that used to bully you?"

Cody nodded. "That was a while ago. That all changed when…" His words fell off as he looked at me, and his facial expressions became sullen. "When Tasha told me how to handle it. She said I should try to befriend him because that was what Bobby needed was a friend. She said he probably didn't know how to make friends. I just wanted to whip his…" He stopped, and a smirk pressed against his lips. "Never mind. But Tasha said that I should be kind to him, and he would come around and wouldn't bully me." He smiled. "It really worked."

I looked at him, and his genuine love and care for Tasha shone through as he spoke about her. I was forced to think about her too. What Tasha had done for him made me love her even more. Who was I kidding? I couldn't love the woman more if I tried. I wanted that love to fade away because I was upset about what showed up in my mailbox, but I was lying to myself if I thought it would. I should have done a better job of listening before I judged her. Looking at the evidence and not the beautiful soul of my woman was a curse of being a lawyer. Now that the blinders were off, I had to talk to Tasha.

Cars behind me began honking for me to move on, so I quickly pulled away from the curb.

En route to our place, Cody broke his silence. "I miss her, Uncle Matt."

I peered at him through the rearview mirror and saw his saddened mood. It had shown up on and off since I explained to him Tasha might not be coming back because we had an argument. Cody didn't talk much about her after that, and I was grateful for that, but now he was ready to discuss his feelings about her being gone.

"You hadn't told me this before, Cody."

"I don't tell you what I think about it because I don't want you to be sad."

"Cody, you can talk to me about her. I miss her too."

His eyes lifted to ensnare mine in the mirror. "Then, why don't you get her back? What happened?"

There was no way I would go into those details with him, so I kept it simple. "A lot of adult stuff," I shot back, looking towards the road.

"Okay…" Cody's voice trailed off, and his forehead wrinkled, so I knew he was thinking about what I'd said, but he didn't say another word about it.

Our talk did make me think I needed to do something more than I expected to do. I had to talk to her because it wasn't doing any of us any good feeling this miserable. Plus, I had to know how she was doing. She was still the woman I loved, and she helped Cody, so that deserved a thank you. I couldn't wait to talk to her. Anticipating seeing her again left me feeling excited.

Chapter Twenty

Tasha

Unexpected Visitor

I quickly got back into the swing of working full-time. I had actually forgotten how much I enjoyed writing. However, even though it was what I enjoyed doing, it was no longer my passion. My heart was elsewhere and remained there.

After finding that the clock had flipped over to four-thirty, I was out of there but was stopped short when I spotted Vicky heading my way.

"Sorry. I know you're cutting out of here, but will you read through this intro? I think it's missing something."

I grabbed the paper from her and read through it. Something definitely was missing, so I quickly jotted down some notes and handed it back to her. "Maybe this sounds better."

She looked at it and smiled, nodding her approval. "Perfect! A stronger opening line and bullet points are exactly what it needed. Thanks, Tasha!" She scurried back to her desk to finish her piece.

I proceeded to head out of the office for a long night of holiday Lifetime movies. I was happy to give corrective ideas and suggestions without criticizing the writers underneath me as Melinda and Nina had done to me, but that was water under the bridge. Pushing through the glass doors, I fished my keys out of my purse and headed towards the car. When I looked back up, the sight before me slowed me down to a turtle's pace. Matt was leaning against my car, eyes trained on me.

"Hey," he said softly. His baritone brought back every memory I tried to suppress over the past few weeks.

"Um…hey… Is everything alright with Cody?" I didn't know why that was my first thought, but it was.

"Yeah, everything is fine with Cody. He's staying with a friend overnight, and I just thought I'd stop by and see how you're doing."

I looked off in the distance, staring at nothing in particular. "I'm fine, Matt."

Matt's warm hand touching my face brought my eyes to his. "I'm glad you're doing alright, Tasha. Joseph told me you started back working as head writer. Congratulations." His low and thick voice could've melted the sun.

"Thanks, Matt, and thank you for everything you did to help me. I appreciate it, and I've been meaning to tell you that." As much as I tried to avoid his piercing eyes that would surely drag me back into his orbit, I couldn't resist the pull to look at him.

"So, here's the thing…I've been doing a lot of thinking and was hoping you could come over so we could talk, or I'll come to your place. If you don't feel comfortable with either of those options, we can go to a restaurant. I just have to talk to you about what happened."

I wasn't so sure going back to the scene of the crime would be such a good idea, and truthfully, I wasn't sure I was ready to face a conversation with Matt. How much could one heart take?

"I've finally gotten to the point where I'm not kicking my own ass about my past, and I'd like to stay that way," I admitted.

"Tasha, I should have given you a chance to explain yourself, and I want to hear what you have to say."

"That's it, Matt. I don't have anything to say to you now. I just feel like we should—"

Matt stepped closer to me, so close that I could hear his breaths as they circulated in his lungs. "Come with me, Tasha. I *need*...to hear you out, which is what I should have done from the beginning."

His nearness made me lose my gumption to fight. Going with him seemed so natural, so right. At one point, I couldn't imagine not going wherever he led me.

"I would like to talk to you, Matt, but I'm not so sure your place or mine would be the best idea. Maybe a restaurant would work."

"Okay. Can I at least pick you up?"

"You can pick me up," I agreed.

He smiled at that small win. "Okay, then, I'll pick you up at seven."

"I'll be ready."

He took my keys from my hand and opened my door for me, helping me inside. Then, he trekked back to his car. He waved as he backed out of his parking space. Watching him leave, my heart raced wildly in my chest. I believed nothing bad could come from talking to him, but I was hesitant. It would break me to have to lose him twice.

***

Matt picked me up, and we rode together to the restaurant. It was all pretty normal, other than there wasn't a kiss greeting, and the ride to the restaurant was pretty quiet. I didn't know what to expect or why I was even there. He didn't say anything, and I was afraid to dive into our discussion.

We got to the restaurant, and it wasn't even until after we ordered that we started a genuine conversation. "So, first off...I need to thank you."

I arched an eyebrow at that statement. "You're thanking me? For what?" I asked after taking a sip from my water glass. For some reason, I felt like my mouth was full of cotton, and I needed something much more than water to quench my thirst. Maybe liquor.

That was when he told me the story about Cody's new friend. "Cody and Bobby are friends, and I don't know how you did that, but it was good to see them walking out of the school together, laughing and talking, just being bros. And from what I hear...that's because of you." There was a twinkle in his eyes as he talked about Cody's new relationship with Bobby.

I was happy, too, but shrugged. "I didn't do anything, not really. It was Cody's responsibility to get Bobby to talk to him, and he did it. Your nephew is an extraordinary little man."

He smiled his usual genuine smile, warming up my insides. I missed it so much that I just sat for a moment and admired the beauty of it. His sparkling white teeth and perfectly shaped lips was coupled with a glow spread across his entire face.

"He is pretty special, but I thought I needed to reach out to you and thank you for giving him the courage to face his

171

fears and conquer them with kindness. You gave him the thought of becoming friends with Bobby. It was genius."

I nodded slowly and looked away from him. All this thanking me had me wondering if the only reason he invited me out was to thank me for doing something so small. "So, that's what this is about?" I asked, motioning my hand toward our dinner. "You just wanted to invite me out to thank me for doing my job? I mean, I was his babysitter at the time, and it's only right that I try to help him be a good human being."

"Well, I suppose you could say that it was just part of your job, but I say that it's a part of who you are. And no, that isn't the only reason I asked you out."

I sat back in my seat as the waitress brought us our food, and we thanked her. Once she was gone, he started to pick at his chicken, but I waited to eat. "Okay, then what other reason is there?" I nudged him to discuss the real reason we were there.

He put down his chicken and wiped off his hands. "I've been thinking, and I realized I wasn't fair to you. I didn't give you a chance to tell me how you ended up in a porn video." His discomfort of talking about the contents of that video was evident in the way his eyes fluttered when he mentioned it.

"No, you didn't," I started but bit my lower lip and scooped a small spoonful of potatoes onto my spoon. I didn't know why I did it because my appetite was gone. I figured this was my psyche's way of stalling the conversation.

"Tasha, I let you walk out of my life... *our* lives without so much as a word from you. That wasn't fair, and I want to correct it now. Tell me what I didn't give you a chance to say that night."

Taking a deep breath while listening to everything I wanted to hear him say from the beginning of this mess, I didn't know where to start, except at the very beginning.

"It happened when I was getting my feet wet as a writer. Getting ready to work on a new story that would put me on the map, I wanted to make a big impression. I hooked up with this guy named Harper Finley to make it happen. He was supposedly able to pitch my story to the *New York Times* and *Washington Post* and get me on as a permanent part of the staff," I paused, feeling the terrible memories of that time in my life all rush back in at once. "What I didn't see coming was me losing my integrity and heart to him."

"So...you fell in love?" he pensively inquired.

"Well, I thought it was love. It turns out that I didn't know then what love truly was. He told me everything I wanted to hear, and I believed him. And then everything fell apart. He didn't have any intention of connecting me with the editors of those prominent newspapers. When we were having sex, he was videotaping me. He asked me to take near-nude photos so he could have memories of me when we weren't together. Shortly after all of that, he humiliated me by leaking the sex tape in a compilation he created called *'What Girls Will Do For Fame'* and then he sold the photos. It became painfully clear that he was only using me."

His face fell as he realized how I had been played and how the same people who played me had pitted him against me. "Oh, wow...Tasha, I'm sorry that happened to you. You don't deserve that; you don't deserve any of this."

I shrugged in an attempt to brush off the hurt that tried to invade the peace I worked so hard to attain. I thought I got past this and didn't even know a DVD still existed. God only knows if it was on the internet. Trying to hold myself together so I wouldn't sob in front of Matt, I said, "There are sharks in the business, and I guess I have a big X on my forehead since I'm always a target."

"Who do you think sent it to me?" he asked furiously.

"Melinda gained access to it when we worked together. She pretended to be outraged about it, and I thought she cared about me at the time. She told me she had gotten rid of the copy she had, but I guess she didn't and thought now would be a good time to dredge it up and get even with me. She lost her job and any hopes of having you, so I figure she sent it to you because she thought at least I would lose the guy, and it worked."

His eyes met mine as he released a sigh. Taking my hand into his, he poured out his heart, "I should have listened to you, especially since this whole thing reeked of Melinda. I should have heard you out. My emotions wouldn't let me think straight. Will you forgive me, baby?"

I wanted to for my own peace of mind and heart, but... "First of all, this isn't your fault, Matt. I'm just sorry it came out the way it did. I would have talked to you about it when I was comfortable, but I never wanted it to be discovered like this by you. But, what happens the next time something unsavory shows up in the mail involving me? I have a past like everyone else does, and I don't want to get kicked out of yours and Cody's life every time you hear or see something bad about me, at least without being able to give my side of things first."

Matt closed his eyes and swallowed hard as if ingesting his emotions and willing them to stay down. "Seeing you with another man nearly drove me insane, even knowing he was before my time." He shook his head as if to drive those images from his mind. Then, slowly, he looped his fingers with mine. "It was a mistake to let you go. You are a good woman, Tasha. I just couldn't remember that when looking at that tape and I'm so sorry for letting you walk away. I knew it was the wrong thing to do seconds after you were gone. I don't want you to go anywhere without me again. I promise I'll listen to your side of things, not make snap decisions, and I could smack Melinda for doing this to you…to *us*."

I could sense the pain he was in and it hurt me as much as it did him. My own pain from losing him was too much. I was going to have to forgive him in order to be free of it, to find a way back to the man I loved who had every right to react the way he did.

Tightening my hold on his fingers, I smiled, trying to put him at ease. "Don't worry about Melinda. She has already gotten her karma, and she may be getting another visit from karma because she obviously didn't learn anything the first time. Let's eat and try to forget about her. She has stolen enough time from us already."

Slipping my hand out of his, he was quick to grab it again to place a kiss on the back of it. The gesture, as small as it was, gave me hope we would soon find our way back to each other.

Chapter Twenty-One

Matt

Restore Me

Tasha having to endure the pain she experienced at the hands of the ass of a man she dated infuriated me. I had been so quick to jump to every wrong conclusion about her, and that upset me even more. If I had to do it all over, I absolutely would have listened to her, but I couldn't take it back. I could only move us forward and hope she would forgive me for not standing by her side when Melinda wronged her again.

We finished off dinner and talked like old times. Tasha was enthusiastic about the new projects she was working on, and I spoke to her about some of my clients. Melinda could have ruined what we shared—easy conversation and understanding—and I would be half responsible because I allowed it.

"I missed this," Tasha said as the conversation slowed down.

"Me too. I missed you, baby. With the way I reacted, I'm no better than the jerk that recorded you."

She shook her head and softly shushed me. "Don't say that, Matt. I understand why you pushed me away. Maybe once we fell for each other, I should have put in a disclaimer that there was damning material out there that could one day come back and haunt us, but I didn't. So sure, I was hurt when you rejected me, but time will mend my feelings. I've just missed not having you there by my side."

"Then, we shouldn't waste another minute." I placed some money down on the table and motioned for her to get up. When she circled the table, I hauled her close to me and wrapped my arm around her. Holding her close as we left the restaurant, we headed back to my car.

Once we reached her door, she turned to me and gazed up into my eyes. "I'm sorry," she whispered.

"No...I'm sorry." I brushed a strand of hair from her face, leaning in to press her against the car as our mouths embraced. Two breaths traveled in and out, becoming one. I loved this woman and needed to get her home to show her just how much.

Her apartment was closer to the restaurant, so I drove us there. Two weeks of missing Tasha had me ready to lose myself in her. Once we got to her apartment, there was a mad dash to her door. As she unlocked it, I whispered into her ear, telling her how beautiful she was to me.

Giggling, she fumbled with her keys in a useless attempt to open the front door. "I'll never figure out how to use my key if you keep talking to me like that."

"If you don't open it, I'll take you right up against this door, and given how much I need you right now, you know I will do it." I snuggled even closer to her allowing her to feel how much I truly missed her.

Her door lock clicked open, and we finally entered the warmth of her apartment. Turning around, she wrapped her arms around me, massaging her fingers through my hair as I pushed her back towards her bedroom, where I devoured her lips like a man struggling for his last breath.

Parting from the kiss, we couldn't wait any longer. Undressing as we moved toward her bed, she grabbed onto her panties, removing the last piece of clothing as she sat on the bed and inched backward, pulling me with her.

"I love you," she softly whispered as my lips touched hers.

Pulling her close to me, I swiped my tongue across her lips. "I love you so much, baby."

She writhed beneath me as I ran my hand over every one of her curves, exploring the succulent paths I remembered so well. Latching onto her neck, I sucked, desperate to taste her delicious flesh. My throbbing cock ached to be buried inside of her when she whimpered and called out my name. Tasha's hands wandered down my back, her fingers gently stroking my muscles.

Tracing her collarbone with my lips, I thought I would go up in a blaze of fire. Moving down to her perky nipples, between my teeth, as her hands ran back up my back, clutching handfuls of my hair, while I enthusiastically indulged in her tasty flesh, almost undid me. As I tugged her right nipple between my teeth, she softly said my name, satisfying my need to hear it on her lips. Longingly, I kissed each areola, swirling my tongue lavishly around. Continuing my descent, I traveled down her stomach, sucking her soft skin with feverish pride. Three kisses along her navel were applied, then I moved further south.

"Matt... Yes..."

Her pussy was so wet that I could see the juices on her nether lips. She spread her legs slowly, allowing me entry to her opening. Spreading her labia open with the pads of my thumb, I slowly stroked her clit. Her trembles let me know she missed me as much as I missed her. Unable to take it any longer, I lowered my face between her thighs and flicked my tongue against her nub.

"Holy fuck, Matt," she moaned, nearly popping up off the bed.

Grabbing ahold of her hips, steadying her as I moved my tongue in and out, I marked my spot while tasting how sweet and wet she was. She was delicious, and I wanted to feast on her until I was full. My tongue gave her no mercy, and she screamed out her pleasure as her pussy began to pulsate against my tongue.

"Yes, Matt…..ahhhh!"

Her juices jetted from her, and I lapped up every ounce of her sweetness.

Falling back against the bed, Tasha gasped for air. Moving up her body, she clawed at my back as we held one another. My engorged cock would explode before I made my entrance if I didn't enter her soon.

Shifting my body until I fell into place, Tasha wrapped her legs around my waist and pulled me into her sanctuary. I sank so deep inside of her that we became one. She grabbed my shoulders, pulling me into a heated kiss. Every shift of her body beneath me caused me more pleasure. Her pussy wrapped around me snugly, so perfectly that I didn't want to ever evacuate.

"Matt, please…" she cried as I pulled out of her core.

I nibbled softly on her ear. "What do you want, baby?" I whispered sweetly.

"I want you!" she cried out. "Please, just give it to me!"

"My pleasure." I placed my lips to hers and insanely kissed her as I entered her wetness, balls deep.

Yelping, she was unable to utter a sound due to me covering her mouth with another intense kiss.

When my release was near, I couldn't stop it if I tried. With a loud growl, I splashed her heated core with my seed. I wanted her to have my children one day, and I was glad we would now have the time to work on our future.

With the truth out in the open, I'd always regret not hearing her side of the story, and I would spend the rest of our lives together making it up to her.

Epilogue

Tasha

Dreams Come True

Four Months Later

I looked at the clock on my computer before logging out. I had to pick Cody up from his friend's house, and I didn't want to be late. Since getting back together with Matt, we had the perfect little arrangement. I worked many of my hours for *Colorful Times* from home, which allowed me to spend a lot of time with Cody. I had the best of both worlds. When I did have to go into the office for a meeting or to show my face, Dana or another of my friends would watch Cody.

Summer had arrived, and Cody wasn't in school, so we got to spend a lot of time together. Matt and I now had an agreement never to walk away upset with one another and to talk over everything. We both learned from our mistakes and had no intention of repeating them, and especially not to allow a third wheel inside of our relationship.

Turning off the lights in my office, I headed through the office building, ready to go home.

"Hey, I'm heading out. Call or text if you need anything," I told Rachel just as I reached the door. Rachel was one of the writers I hired, and she was doing an excellent job on her column.

"Will do, Tasha. Have a good afternoon!"

181

Walking through the building, I smiled, feeling high on life. Then, I spotted Melinda heading straight towards me.

"Melinda Lory," I stated with disdain dripping from my tone. "To what do we owe this surprise?"

She rolled her eyes. "Hello, Tasha. Long time, no see."

After sending the DVD to Matt, she seemed to go off the radar. Months without seeing her had me grateful, but now she was here in the flesh.

"What are you doing here, Melinda? You don't work here anymore, so what do you want?"

She laughed sarcastically. "Let's just say I missed the place."

"Ha. Really?"

"I do miss it, but my real reason for being here is to see how you are doing... with the porno video and all," she sniped.

"Well, that's sweet of you. Perhaps you wanted to see if Matt and I were still together. Well, yes, we are, and there is nothing you can do about it."

She narrowed her eyes into slits. "Don't worry, Tasha. You don't have to tell me what's going on with you two…I already know. I've seen that you are still together and going strong." She moved closer to me and glowered as she continued, "I have eyes everywhere, you know? But really, I wanted to apologize for sending him that video of you. As much as I wanted to break you two apart, I shouldn't have done that."

I raised an eyebrow, trying to understand which angle Melinda was shooting from this time around.

"You…apologize? That's something I never thought I'd live to see. What's the catch?"

"No catch. I did some awful things and all for a guy that never even showed me any interest. Don't get me wrong. He's a great guy, but I can admit defeat. And that's what I'm doing."

"Well, forgive me if I don't trust this to be a genuine apology," I fired back. After all, she never apologized for stealing my work and firing me, but for some unknown reason, she had an apology for sending the DVD to Matt.

"I understand that. But sitting at home for months without a job gave me plenty of time to think about the things I've done wrong. It used to be funny to see people in messed up situations until that person became me."

Melinda honestly looked like she learned a lesson. Still, I waited for the other shoe to fall; this wasn't the Melinda I knew.

"You won the guy, and got the job, and you deserve both, so I'll back off."

"Well, pardon me for being skeptical, because I am," I admitted.

"You don't have to be, Tasha. I mean it. I'm not going to try any more funny business. If Matt is happy with you, then I'll have to accept that and move on." She hesitated before she continued, "Did you hear I got a writing job in Atlanta?"

"No, I haven't heard about it."

"It's not as lucrative as my old job, but it's a great career move, and I could use the change in scenery. So, I'm moving out of Florida and backing off, and I'm serious."

As much as I didn't want to believe her, what she was saying seemed sincere.

"Thanks, Melinda, for at least coming up here to say that to me."

"And thank you for allowing me to apologize."

I turned to walk away but then turned back around to face her. "Good luck with your new job, Melinda." Luck was more than she afforded me, but it seemed like the right thing to say.

"Thank you, Tasha. And good luck to you too, Miss Head Writer." She smiled genuinely, turned, and headed toward the exit.

I stood in the same spot for a few minutes, wondering if I'd just dreamed Melinda up. Was Melinda Lory turning a new leaf?

***

I pulled up in front of the house to pick Cody up and got out of my car. Matt's motorcycle pulled up, and he took his helmet off and glanced my way. As he got off the bike, I stepped to the curb. "What are you doing here? I thought you were working today?"

"Hop on," he said, reaching behind him and handing me the second helmet.

I tilted my head and looked at the serene smile on Matt's face; it didn't match the anxiety building inside of me. "I know you don't think I'm about to ride that thing, and where is Cody?"

He grabbed my hand and pulled me to him. His lips softly touched mine. I placed my hand to his chest, melting against him until we broke from the intimate kiss.

"Everything is taken care of, Tasha. Dana is watching Cody today."

"Why? I'm here."

Matt pointed to the back of his motorcycle. "Get on, Tasha."

"Can I ride behind you in my car?" I pouted.

"No, leave it here. It's time you got broken in on the bike, anyway."

"Broke and bike should not ever be said in the same sentence when you're trying to convince someone to ride with you, Matt." But, there was something he wasn't telling me and he wasn't going to, so I sucked up my reluctance and allowed him to help me onto the back of the bike.

Wrapping my arms around him, I nestled into his back as he drove off. The wind blew through my hair, and surprisingly, it felt awesome to breeze through traffic, holding onto my man. I had no idea where he was taking me, but it didn't matter.

After riding for almost an hour, we turned into a long driveway. Matt stopped the bike at someone's farm, but it didn't seem as if they were around. I took my helmet off and slid off the bike.

"Where are we?"

He beamed like a schoolboy with a secret. "My family's farm."

He had been so secretive about his family, so that admission was a shock to me. "Your family owns this?"

He nodded. "It always seemed too big for just me and Cody; that's why we don't stay here. I have someone to keep it up for me."

Smiling, I looked around the place in awe. On a portion of the impressive property, there was a moderate-looking brown house. The land was beautiful, with acres and acres of green grass for as far as the eye could see. "This place is beautiful, Matt." I was so awestruck by the serene surroundings that I couldn't say more.

Matt walked around to the back of his motorcycle and pulled out a wicker basket I hadn't noticed before. "I hope you're hungry."

"You packed us lunch?" I moved closer to him and knotted my hands around his neck to pull him into a kiss. I couldn't be any more in love with him than I was at that moment.

"Yes, baby. And with that type of affection as a reward, I'm glad I did."

As we ate, he pointed out various parts of his grandparent's farm, places he liked to hang out when he was growing up. We sat on a blanket, next to a pond, where he told me his sister taught him to swim, and his mother taught him to fish. It was so refreshing that I didn't want the day to end when we finished eating and loaded the basket with what we didn't eat.

"You said you wanted to discuss something with me. What is it about?"

"Your job."

"My job as your sitter or my writing job?"

"It's about the sitting job. Well, I don't think it's going to work out with you being my babysitter anymore."

"But, who's going to take care of Cody? What made you come to this decision?" I was sure the confusion I felt was written all over my face. Where was Matt going with this? "I'm the best darn babysitter you could have. Are you firing me, Mr. Matthew Wilde?"

Glaring at me for using his surname, he continued, "I have to let you go from that position because …" He scooted closer to me so that he was inches away from my face. "…I have a much bigger job in mind for you, Tasha."

My eyes stayed on his, locked in a state of confusion when his mouth curved into a smile. "What am I missing, Matt? I'm not following you."

When Matthew Wilde adjusted his body to kneel on one knee, reached in his pocket, and retrieved a small, red box, I had to steady myself. Lowering my eyes to the box, I stared at the beautiful diamond ring inside in shock. *Oh my...oh God...oh me.*

"You can't be Cody's babysitter any longer because I want you to be his aunt and my wife. Marry me, and make Cody and me the two luckiest men in the world."

I didn't even hesitate in my answer, "Yes! Yes! Yes! I will marry you."

Matt slipped the ring onto my finger, and it fit perfectly. Standing to his feet, he drew me into his arms, twirled me around, and thanked me for accepting his proposal.

I giggled my heart out, gazing down at the engagement ring. Matt tilted my head up then gripped the sides of my face and covered my mouth with his. This was a kiss I felt in the depths of my heart. Feeling like this with Matt was something I never wanted to end, and now that I had his infinity ring on my finger, I could count on sharing many more kisses like this. Just the thought of spending the rest of my days with him and

Cody was more than I could have imagined in my wildest dreams.

THE END

Dear Reader,

Tasha and Matt are two wrecking balls coming at each other fast. I hope you enjoyed their story. Thanks for staying on the journey for one more story in the Breathless series.

As always, I want to make your reading experience the best possible, but to do that, I need your feedback!

Will you write a review of Breathless 6: Drive Me Wilde on Goodreads and/or Amazon?

Until Next Time...

Best,

Shani

Full Catalog listed at www.shanigreenedowdell.com.

Have you read the *Top 100 Amazon bestseller*, Taken by the Billionaire?

Made in the USA
Columbia, SC
14 April 2022

58947987R00104